CW00727509

Memories of the Dead

A Clara Fitzgerald Mystery

Evelyn James

Red Raven Publications 2023
www.sophie-jackson.com

Contents

Chapter One

It was an icy January day and there was a woman huddled in the doorway of the office. Clara noticed that she wasn't wearing gloves and wondered why someone, so otherwise well-dressed, would miss such a necessity in this weather. She approached closer and the woman looked up.

"May I help you?" Clara offered.

"Oh no dear, I am waiting for Mr C. Fitzgerald."

Clara resisted the temptation to look affronted.

"I am *Miss* C. Fitzgerald and this is my office."

"*You* are a private investigator?" The woman looked flustered.

"Indeed and I take it you are waiting for me?"

The woman was still stunned and then her face fell.

"I do apologise, I assumed you were something to do with that establishment," she motioned with her eyes to the next doorway which led into a haberdasher's. Clara rented the rooms above the shop for her office space, which usually worked very well, especially as it had its own private entrance. But sometimes it caused confusion, as was happening right now with the strange woman in the doorway who was beginning to look quite distressed.

"Shall we go upstairs and discuss whatever you came to see me about?" Clara was feeling grumpy that morning, Tommy had had another bad night, and she didn't feel in the mood to explain her unusual career choice on the cold doorstep, "I can pop the kettle on as soon as we get up there and warm us up a bit. Your hands look frozen."

"Oh, yes," the woman seemed to notice her hands for the first time as she moved aside to let Clara unlock the door. "I was in such a hurry to get here that I must have forgotten my gloves. It's urgent, you see."

Clara refrained from saying that rarely people visited her with problems that were not urgent and motioned for her to go inside.

The staircase was dark in the narrow hall; no one had seen the need to furnish it with gas lighting when the other rooms were modernised, so Clara kept a stubby candle on a shelf by the door to light her way. Clara drew some matches from her pocket and lit the candle before ushering her guest ahead of her. The woman began to talk nervously as they climbed the stairs.

"I am Mrs Wilton, forgive my poor introduction. I have never visited a detective before and didn't expect a woman, though these days, I suppose, one should be quite prepared for such events. I found your name in the classifieds, it said you had done some good service for the Mayor of Brighton and I thought to myself that must count for something."

"You would think, Mrs Wilton," Clara opened the first door on the landing which led to the front of the apartment and was arranged as her office.

There was a big old desk in front of the window, rather dominating the room, and a small chair before it for clients. At the back of the room, just behind the door, was a grand old sofa which Clara termed her 'thinking spot' but which equally served as a day-bed to catch up on her sleep when Tommy was going through one of his bad spells with the night terrors. Close to hand was a bookcase, mostly used as a rudimentary filing system, and an old fireplace with a small stove tucked in one corner where Clara could boil a kettle if she wished.

Clara pulled off her mackintosh and her grey hat and hung them on a hook on the wall. She attempted to take Mrs Wilton's coat but the woman was too distracted to notice.

"Please take a seat." Clara indicated the chair before the desk and left Mrs Wilton hovering by it while she lit the stove and went to the back room to fill the kettle with water. When she returned, the stove was just beginning to generate some warmth and she left the kettle standing on it before taking her own seat behind the desk. She noticed Mrs Wilton was studying the only painting on the otherwise barren walls.

"My father's portrait. He was a doctor," Clara explained.

"I would think you would keep such a sentimental piece at home," Mrs Wilton asked curiously.

"My brother prefers it here, we lost both our parents during the war and he finds it hard to have pictures around."

"I understand," Mrs Wilton suddenly looked serious. "I lost my husband and son in the war."

"I am sorry."

"Oh, it's not exactly novel these days, is it? You are more unique not to have lost someone."

"Still, it is hard."

Both ladies were silent for an instant contemplating their own losses.

"I suppose that is why I came here," Mrs Wilton broke the mood. "It is all to do with my husband."

"I'm afraid I have had little success trying to trace what happened to men who died in action, though I am often asked."

"It's not that. I may not know where the bodies of my husband and son lie, but I know their souls are safely in Glory, that doesn't concern me."

"That is good," Clara gave her best sympathetic smile. "Too many women feel they cannot rest until they know where a loved one died and was buried. It can quite destroy them. So, what is your situation?"

"Well... may I take it that whatever I say is confidential?"

"As if it was said in a confessional, though I don't offer absolution." Mrs Wilton smirked.

"I find I am not the confessing type, normally anyway, I don't go in for all that Catholic stuff. I'm a Spiritualist. Have you heard of us?"

"You believe it is possible to communicate with the dead."

"As a crude assessment of our beliefs, yes. Look Miss Fitzgerald, I need to know you will listen to what I have to say with an open mind."

Clara felt her suspicions rising; she was not in the mood for games and was starting to think Mrs Wilton was wasting her time.

"I am reasonably open-minded, Mrs Wilton, though I would not make the mistake of taking that to mean I am gullible."

"Of course not! It's just some people will laugh at one when you talk about the afterlife and so forth."

"I would not laugh, but I do need a physical case to work on. Spiritual problems are out of my area of expertise."

"I'm not so foolish," Mrs Wilton bristled a little, then visibly deflated. "It's about money, which, I am sure, is perfectly in your area of expertise."

Clara was offended but prudently held her tongue.

"If you explain your situation I shall see what I can do."

"It is simple really. My husband was old-fashioned in his thinking and could not abide banks. He promised me before he went to the Front that he had left me a sizeable sum of money, should the worst happen, to safeguard my future," Mrs Wilton paused and fiddled nervously with the clutch on her bag. "Only it seems he didn't."

"Didn't?"

"Leave me any money."

"He left no will?"

"Not to my knowledge and I have hunted for it. He didn't trust solicitors either, you see. So life has been rather difficult for me as you can imagine. I have had to dismiss most of the servants, and I have been making ends meet by selling whatever I can, but even that has been hard in this day and age."

"I quite understand, Mrs Wilton," Clara said, and she did too, many families had been left destitute by the loss of a bread winner in the war. She, herself, only just made ends meet with her 'little detective business', as some critics were cruel enough to call it. "But I am still not clear on what you want from me?"

"It has been very hard," Mrs Wilton continued, as though she had not quite heard Clara. "And after a while you can't mask things. People notice. Even you."

"Me, Mrs Wilton?"

"You spotted my gloves were missing. I simply don't have a pair without holes in them to wear, and I suppose my pride got the better of me, so I would rather freeze my fingers off in the middle of winter then let you see me wearing shabby gloves."

Clara unconsciously glanced at her own worn mackintosh, how she wished she could buy a new one, but at least her pride had not moved her to discard it entirely in favour of freezing to death.

"Pride is cheap, my mother used to say," Mrs Wilton sighed heavily. "I think she meant that everyone could afford to have some in themselves, but I wonder now if she was really quite wrong. Pride can actually cost a person quite a lot."

"Would you like a cup of tea?" Clara interrupted as the kettle started to faintly whistle. She decided it was time to move the conversation on before Mrs Wilton became too maudlin. She was beginning to feel rather sorry for the woman and knew that was not a good sign as she would be tempted to drop her rates sympathetically, or worse, offer to do the work for free. Tommy would never let her hear the end of it if she did.

"Yes please," Mrs Wilton nodded.

Clara fidgeted with the boiling water and an old brown teapot which had a spout half-clogged with old tea leaves. Nestling it in a striped knitted cosy she brought it to the table and spent a while longer finding a matching pair of cups and saucers. The whole procedure perhaps took a little under ten minutes, enough time, as Clara poured out the tea, for Mrs Wilton to gather herself together and remember what she was there for. Clara slipped a cup of weak tea in front of her.

"Ignore the tea leaves, I can't remember where I left the strainer."

"Thank you," Mrs Wilton warmed her hands on the cup.

"So," Clara said sipping her tea thoughtfully, "let's get to the gist of this problem. Why are you here?"

Mrs Wilton dragged her teaspoon around her cup as though the action could help her summon up the strength to talk.

"I explained that people begin to notice these things and servants, especially dismissed servants, talk. I was taken to one side at a church service by a dear lady in her nineties who is a very ardent spiritualist and, well, I suppose I was just so unhappy that a kind word or two had me sobbing on her shoulder. I told her what I told you, and she felt I would benefit from a private reading, and then the following week she brought me this card," Mrs Wilton withdrew a thin slip of white cardboard from her purse and anxiously passed it to Clara.

The card simply read: Mrs. Martha Greengage, Spiritualist Medium, 261 Chestnut Grove, Brighton. Clara read the card and then looked at her client.

"I know what you must think, a gullible old woman desperate for answers and clutching at straws," Mrs Wilton's voice trembled. "But, believe me, I was sceptical too. Going to a spiritualist church is one thing, but I have always been a little suspicious of private clairvoyants. It really was only because of this dear old lady that I was convinced to go at all. She told me that Mrs Greengage specialised in lost property and had even helped someone in the nobility to retrieve a small lost fortune, and I really was at the end of my tether by that point, actually I still am."

Mrs. Wilton gave a painful laugh. Clara laid down the card, her heart even more drawn to the poor woman who had put her last hopes in a charlatan (Clara had no doubts that was exactly what Mrs Greengage was) who almost certainly charged a fortune. She took a moment to think through what she should say next and kept her expression carefully neutral as she spoke.

"What was Mrs Greengage like?"

"Old and," Mrs Wilton hesitated, "a bit 'witchy' for my likes. She wears a lot of black, though I believe Mr Greengage is alive and well, and she keeps a white parrot that she claims is also sensitive and is sometimes possessed by visiting spirits. She didn't inspire confidence on my first visit to be honest."

"You don't strike me as a foolish woman Mrs Wilton, but I take it from your tone you have visited this woman more than once?"

"Oh yes, at least five times."

"And because of these visits you are now here?"

Mrs Wilton blinked.

"Oh dear, I don't think I have made myself very clear. You see, I was sceptical on that first visit but after what I saw I could hardly remain so. Mrs Greengage really does have a gift."

Chapter Two

"I seem to be no closer to understanding how I may help you?" Mrs Wilton sighed.

"I have to explain this a little more logically. I went to visit Mrs Greengage on a Friday night about a month ago with the dear lady who gave me the card. To her credit Mrs Greengage did not charge me anything for that first visit which is more than can be said for most businesses."

"My consultations are free also," Clara interrupted gently.

"Well that is because you are a woman, dear, and women understand that not everything requires money up-front. A little chat should always be free," Mrs Wilton took a sip of her tea. "Where was I? Oh yes, Mrs Greengage opened her door looking like some sort of witch out of a pantomime and I was quite astounded. Did I mention she had a red carnation in her hair?"

"No," Clara said, having a hard time keeping a straight face as the image of Mrs Greengage began to form in her mind.

"Really it is ridiculous in a woman that age. I suppose it is all for show," Mrs Wilton tutted. "As you can imagine, I wondered what sort of a place I had been brought to, but she was polite enough and it seemed churlish to walk away when I had been invited."

Mrs Wilton leaned forward in her chair.

"She escorted us into her front parlour the likes of which I have not seen since my grandmother was alive. Not a modern thing in sight and all the furniture dark and heavy and all these statues everywhere of classical figures. Some were so indiscreet in their apparel I hardly knew where to look," Mrs Wilton's eyes went wide. "And then there was the parrot, sitting on a perch in the middle of this green-draped table with these awful beady eyes peering at you. I was quite unnerved, the thing looked possessed."

"I fear that is a common state with parrots," Clara answered, before her client continued.

"Mrs Greengage had us sit at the table and for my benefit explained she was a medium and the parrot sometimes channelled spirits. Just as she said that the awful bird looked straight at me and went 'Dorothy!' Well that's my Christian name and I was so stunned to hear it I nearly fell out of my seat. Mrs Greengage looked at me then and said, 'There is a spirit wants to speak to you, Mrs Wilton, it's a man and his name is Geoffrey'."

"Your husband," Clara concluded.

"Oh no, I don't know any Geoffrey. Well except the baker's little boy, but he was hardly likely to be channelling himself through a parrot!"

Clara felt the realm of things 'hardly likely' to happen had already been seriously breached.

"No, no, Geoffrey was some sort of spirit mediator – a go-between," Mrs Wilton continued. "It seems Geoffrey had been in contact with my husband in the afterlife. I'm still a bit hazy about how it all came about, perhaps there is some sort of giant meeting place up there. Anyway Geoffrey had spoken with Arthur, my husband, and promised that if I stuck with Mrs Greengage, Arthur would eventually be able to come through in person, but in the meantime Geoffrey would relay the messages."

"Ah," said Clara beginning to see the game unfold. "So you 'stuck' with Mrs Greengage?"

"I had to! Geoffrey said Arthur was desperate to speak with me but was gathering his strength. Apparently it takes a while for a spirit to properly disengage itself from the corporeal world and, until it does, communication is very difficult."

"How many sessions did it take for Mr Wilton to gather his strength?" Clara guessed enough to make a shilling or two.

"It was the fourth session he came through, I believe."

"Via the parrot?"

"Sort of, you see a bird has a limited vocabulary, as Mrs Greengage puts it, so she listens to the parrot psychically and then tells us."

"Right, but Mr Wilton eventually came through?"

"Yes."

"And he said?"

"He was deeply upset by the situation I found myself in, felt it was all his fault for not being clearer about where the money was. He promised he would help, but it would take him time to gather enough spiritual force to get the information to me. I was desperate, as you can imagine and could hardly wait, thinking soon all my prayers would be answered," Mrs Wilton had started to tremble with emotion. "Then, last night when I arrived, Mrs Greengage was bubbling with excitement. Arthur had visited her in her sleep and had caused her to dream of this vivid map, which, when she awoke, she felt compelled to draw out."

Mrs Wilton fiddled in her handbag again and took out a folded piece of paper. Opening it, she showed it to Clara, who saw it was a blotchy map drawn in red ink and loosely recognisable as the outskirts of Brighton.

"That's my house," Mrs Wilton pointed to a coloured square. "And these are landmarks; the field, the church and the duck pond. Arthur told Mrs Greengage that he had buried all of his wealth in a tea chest and this map would lead me to it."

Clara took the map and studied it. It was rudimentary and lacked any indications of roads, directions or even the compass points. It looked like something a child would scribble and hardly helpful to the desperate woman across from her.

"You are wondering about directions? Arthur was very security conscious and created clues to help locate the treasure. He wrote nine and the first three he told me the same night Mrs Greengage gave me the map. He is going to give me another three next week when I visit and the last in a fortnight's time. It is very clear."

"That it is," Clara nodded, impressed by the ingenuity, though not the ethics, of Mrs Greengage.

"And now perhaps you can see where you come in?" Mrs Wilton smiled hopefully.

"Not entirely," Clara answered though she had a strong suspicion.

"Why, I want you to translate the clues and find the treasure for me! You see the clues are riddles," Mrs Wilton handed over a handful of papers, each with writing in the same distinct red ink.

Clara repressed a sigh; she really didn't like riddles or wild goose chases.

"I have to ask, Mrs Wilton, is this sort of thing something your husband was likely to do?"

Mrs Wilton looked puzzled.

"What do you mean, dear?"

"I am curious if he was the sort of man to whom riddles and treasure hunts appealed."

"Does that matter?"

Clara bit her lip and looked at the slips of paper. She was sensing this would prove a delicate moment.

"I was just wondering whether our spiritual personas were much the same as our physical ones."

It was a fumbled answer, but Mrs Wilton seemed satisfied.

"He quite liked acrostic rhymes, though I must say he was never very good at them."

"So it might have pleased his..." Clara shut her eyes as the next sentence formed unerringly on her lips, "...spirit, to write little riddles?"

"I think so, yes," Mrs Wilton suddenly flushed. "I know most people think I am a fool who has fallen into the clutches of a charlatan. But I have seen things, heard the things she has said and I can't think of any logical explanation for them other than that she is in contact with the deceased. If you came to a séance you would see for yourself, surely that would not be too much to ask before you turn down this case? Because you are considering turning me down, aren't you?"

Clara saw the desperation on Mrs Wilton's face and her resolve crumbled a bit more. Was it so far-fetched after all that a woman so grief-stricken and in dire need would turn to what seemed the only source of hope, even if it was an old lady with a parrot?

But this Mrs Greengage was a con-artist, she had to be, and she was exploiting a woman's emotional state to make easy money. Even worse, she was taking advantage not of a wealthy woman who had more money than sense, but someone who had to do without coal or bread just to afford another séance. And if Clara took on the case based on these ghostly riddles would she be any better? She would be being paid to investigate something that was impossible.

"I have a special séance booked for tomorrow night and I have reserved a place for a guest. Will you come?" Mrs Wilton persisted.

"Are you absolutely certain that your husband left behind some sort of legacy?"

"Yes, of course!"

"And there is no traceable bank account?"

"Nothing, I already told you."

"You have to forgive me," Clara said sincerely, "but these days it is rare for a person to bury their 'treasure', so to speak."

"Yet my husband did, I am certain of it, and now he is trying to get in touch with me. Please will you come? Let Mrs Greengage prove herself to you."

Clara sighed.

"I need to think about this, Mrs Wilton, it is, you must agree, a very unusual situation."

"I know and I am grateful you have listened to me without laughter or ridicule."

Clara felt even worse now.

"I will think this over and let you know my decision tomorrow. Do you have access to a telephone?"

"I can use the public phone at Mrs Branbury's bakery on the corner. She lets people use it by appointment, usually between twelve and one."

"Then I will ring you then, what is the number?"

"Brighton 42," Mrs Wilton said quickly. "I shall be there waiting and I hope it is good news I hear."

"I make no promises Mrs Wilton," Clara stood to see her client out.

"I'll just have to have a little faith then," Mrs Wilton gave a slight smile. "I'll hear from you tomorrow."

"Of course, but please don't get your hopes up. This is not my usual sort of case."

They said goodbye on the doorstep and Mrs Wilton hurried away up the road, gloveless hands tucked under her arms. The sky had turned ominously grey and a thin veil of snow was beginning to fall. Clara hoped the luckless Mrs Wilton would make it home before the weather turned worse.

She returned to her office and stared at the odd slips of paper left behind by Mrs Wilton, as soft thuds of snow hit the window pane behind her. The riddles were the usual random clues, the like of which Clara remembered from childhood adventure novels. One read;

Think of me before you sleep, where I am lost the earth runs deep.

Another stated;

You'll need me now your world is lost, I am by the steeple and the cross.

And the last one was even more cryptic;

Three paces North, three paces South, the staring man who has no mouth.

Clara imagined Mrs Greengage had spent an enjoyable afternoon working those rhymes out. How the woman kept a straight face when telling them to Mrs Wilton she did not know.

Suddenly she felt very angry. What right did this 'soothsayer' and witch have to convince the poor Mrs Wilton that her husband was in contact and that soon her money woes would be over? She had half a mind to visit the séance just so she could tell Mrs Greengage exactly what she thought of her. But that would mean giving false hope to Mrs Wilton and she couldn't do that. No, she would ring her the next day and tell her she could not take on the case and it would all be over. It wouldn't be a pleasant conversation but it was the only thing she could ethically do.

She neatly stored the riddles and map away in an envelope ready to return to Mrs Wilton and then found some paperwork to finish out of a desperate need to do something to distract herself.

Chapter Three

Tommy was sat in his wheelchair at the dining room table attacking white paper with a pair of scissors. Since the war which had stripped him of the use of his legs he had relied more and more on creative mental activities to, as he put it, keep himself sane. Clara walked in and kissed her older brother's cheek fondly.

"What are these?" She picked up a spiky shard of paper dotted with irregular holes.

"Christmas decos," Tommy replied jovially. "They taught us how to make these in the hospital. Keeps a fellow's mind busy."

"Christmas has been over for two weeks," Clara reminded him as she browsed through an assortment of paper scrapes, some were vaguely recognisable as snowflakes, others defied interpretation.

"I'm preparing for next year," Tommy told her haughtily. "I made a string of angels for the bannister."

Tommy rummaged through the piles of paper and withdrew a string of distorted figures.

"Oh good," Clara said uncertainly. "But couldn't they have been, well, a little more angelic and a little less... demonic?"

Tommy gave her a hard look and then grinned.

"Are they that bad? I did go at it rather hammer and tongs. Needed to distract myself after last night," he frowned apologetically. "Sorry about that, by the way, old thing."

"You didn't do it on purpose," Clara shrugged.

"Bad enough those dreams keep me awake without inflicting it on someone else," Tommy toyed with a lopsided snowflake. "What's up anyway? You look like you have the world on your shoulders."

Clara flopped down into an easy-chair by the fireplace.

"What do you make of Spiritualism, Tommy?"

"Is that the one where you spend all your time talking with the dead?"

"I don't think you do it all day long, but it's a part of what they believe, yes."

"I always thought it an interesting idea," Tommy mused. "Imagine being able to talk to anyone from the past you wanted to, like Aristotle. Though you would have to learn ancient Greek of course."

"They seem to only get in touch with the recently deceased and people they know... knew, I mean," Clara pulled off her shoes and rubbed her toes. "I thought you would be more of a sceptic."

"Me? Oh I know some took the trenches as first class proof God didn't exist, but I wasn't one of them, not that I am about to join the spiritualists and go talking to ma and pa, that is."

"To me it just all seems wishful thinking," Clara sighed.

"There was a lad in the trenches who claimed to see an angel. He had caught a mine in No Man's Land and we only managed to drag back his top half. He lasted an hour like that and, towards the end, he said this angel was coming for him, he could see it," Tommy picked up his string of deformed angels. "We tried to get him to describe the angel, but he couldn't. No one even thought of arguing with him about what he was seeing. Right then it seemed perfectly logical. Of course now we are back to calling things like that hallucinations."

Clara watched her brother tear the string of angels into tiny pieces. Sometimes she tried to imagine being surrounded by dying men, some so horrendously mutilated there was barely anything of them left. But her mind couldn't wrap itself around the thought, which was perhaps just as well considering the nightmares Tommy suffered.

"What's this all about Clara?" Tommy looked up at her sharply.

"I had a new client this morning, she has been visiting a clairvoyant who claims to be in touch with her deceased husband and is feeding her riddles, of all things, to some sort of treasure her husband supposedly buried before he went to war."

"Really? Even I'm not that gullible. What does she want with you?"

"To solve the riddles so she can find the treasure," Clara rooted in her bag and pulled out the envelope of papers.

Tommy inspected each one carefully in turn.

"Who writes in red ink?"

"Clairvoyants. Apparently."

After examining the slips Tommy handed them back to his sister.

"Are you taking the case?" He asked.

"Of course not, this medium is a fraud and I would be one too if I followed clues I knew to be false."

"On the other hand you could take the job and prove the medium a liar, whilst also looking to see if there was any truth to the husband's treasure."

"I would be wasting my client's money and time," Clara rubbed at her eyes wearily. "She wants to believe so badly that her husband left her some money somewhere. She is struggling and I think she has pinned her last hopes on this clairvoyant and a mythical treasure."

"Well that decides it."

"Beg your pardon?"

"If you don't help her she'll find someone else, someone who has no scruples about wasting her money on a wild goose chase, meanwhile she will also still be paying for a medium to tell her lies. You need to step in, prove the clairvoyant a charlatan and find out if there are any legitimate savings left for the poor woman."

It was a persuasive argument and Clara saw the sense in Tommy's words. Besides, if she let Mrs Wilton carry on being fooled when she might be able to help, then she was little better than Mrs Greengage.

"I've got another argument for you," Tommy said fixing her with his brown-eyed stare. "You need the money and I need something other than paper angels to keep my brain going. It's over a month since the mayor's case."

There was truth to that too. Finding cases was never easy when you were a relatively unknown detective; finding a case when you were an unknown female detective was even harder.

Clara had started her business out of the ashes of the Great War. It was partly practical and partly a means to, as Tommy had pointed out, help keep her older brother occupied. It began by helping friends and neighbours who were dealing with the aftermath of losing all their menfolk. Some were still looking for answers as to what had become of loved ones, others were trying to track down lost savings accounts or war pensions. Before she knew it, Clara was the person people went to when they wanted something sorted out.

As she gained a reputation work mounted up, as did the difficulty of the cases she was involved in. She was starting to feel overwhelmed at the same time as Tommy came out of the military hospital in the depths of depression. She had given him some odd research to do just to occupy his mind while she was out of the house and before long he was intrigued by his sister's new life and wanting to know more.

Now, two years on, they were a real partnership, but Tommy still suffered the worst when there was no work to do.

"Think of it this way," Tommy said to her now. "If she was looking for a relative lost in France you would tell her it was a near enough impossible task, but that you would try anyway. Is this so different?"

"She is certain her husband left her money somewhere," Clara admitted.

"Then find it and expose the fraud this medium is conducting!"

Clara closed her eyes for a moment and let her thoughts swirl inside her mind. Mrs Wilton needed someone's help, no doubt about that, and to leave her in the clutches of Mrs Greengage was unthinkable. She opened her eyes having made up her mind.

"I am to ring her tomorrow and I will tell her I will take the case."

"Good."

"But I will charge no fee unless I find her husband's lost savings."

"Clara," Tommy groaned, "you can't give your help away like that. We have our own finances to think about."

"Daddy's investments will see us through, so where is the problem?"

Tommy shook his head at her.

"What were you saying about gullible?"

"I call it being ethical. Now, she has arranged a séance especially for me tomorrow night, I imagine you will want to come?"

"Absolutely!"

"Then I shall ensure you have a place. There. Now I best see if Annie has managed to arrange some dinner."

Tommy grinned at her.

"This is going to be a fun one," he said.

"I hope not, I remember the last case you described as fun. It made me crave dull and boring."

"Just don't get spooked if any ghosts or ghoulies turn up tomorrow night," Tommy mocked.

"Hah!" Clara said as she opened the door. "Don't you worry about me big brother. It's Mrs Greengage who will need to be watching out tomorrow night!"

Mrs Wilton was elated when Clara rang and agreed to come to the séance, she didn't even make a fuss when Clara insisted she would need a second invite for her brother to come along too.

Clara had just hung up the phone receiver, feeling rotten about the whole situation, when the front door opened and Tommy appeared, his chair being pushed by their housemaid Annie.

"Where have you been? It's bitter outside," Clara heard the sharpness of her tone and regretted it. She had been so protective of Tommy since he had come home, but she knew she was beginning to drive everyone crazy, especially herself.

"Hold your hat, old thing," Tommy grinned. "Annie just wheeled this old crock down to the library, that's all. It only opens for two hours on a Wednesday, remember?"

Clara mentally kicked herself. Tommy had told her last night he was going to go to the local lending library and see what books they had on spiritualism.

"Any luck?" Clara asked, casting an apologetic smile at Annie – their one and only servant, regular dogs-body and loyal friend – who seemed to spend most of her time making sure Tommy had everything he needed. She winked back at Clara, a reminder that they were old enough friends for her to know when nerves had gotten the better of her mistress' tongue.

"Did you find anything good?" Clara asked making a determined effort to change the subject.

"A couple of titles. *'From Darkness to Light: a Re-evaluation of Christianity and Spiritualism'*, and *'Essays on the Spiritualist Church and its role in Mediumship'*."

"Sounds quite riveting."

"Well, at least I have something for when I can't sleep and I did pop into Mrs. Eaton's bookshop and pick up a couple of pamphlets on clairvoyance."

Tommy handed over two slim volumes.

"*'The Art of Mediumship'*, and *'Thirty Short Lessons Designed to Strengthen the Mind and Promote Clairvoyant Abilities'*. Should I be worried?"

"I doubt it. It seems mostly to consist of shouting 'is anybody there?' a lot."

Clara gave him back the books.

"Well our places are booked against my better judgement."

"Aren't you excited to be rooting out a potential charlatan?"

"Potential? For certain she is a charlatan."

"Not necessarily, on page 5 of *'Thirty Lessons'* it clearly states that 'certainty' is only a relative state of mind and once we open our minds to impossibilities we will realise there is nothing certain about certainty."

Clara gave him a withering look and Tommy began to laugh.

"If Mrs Greengage starts spouting nonsense like that I may have trouble holding my tongue."

"Keep strong, old thing." Tommy chuckled, "We are doing this for the sake of a destitute widow."

"Yes, yes. Well I have one absolute certainty for you, I am in desperate need of a cup of tea." Clara replied.

"That I will happily concur with."

Chapter Four

Mrs Greengage's house was a middle terrace with thick green drapes and a rusty door knocker in the shape of a lion's head. Clara and Tommy arrived a few minutes before seven and politely waited outside the door until it was opened by a robust lady dressed all in black. She had a slight squint and observed them through a pair of gold-rimmed glasses.

"Clara and Thomas Fitzgerald." Clara offered her hand to shake but Mrs Greengage didn't move.

"You're a little early," she huffed.

Clara resisted the urge to look at her watch which she knew would be registering five to seven. She wasn't quite sure how to reply but fortunately Mrs. Greengage filled the silence.

"You better come in. We are in the parlour on the far left," Mrs Greengage bustled down the corridor without offering to help Clara negotiate the front step with Tommy's wheelchair.

"I don't like her already," she grumbled.

"Really? And she seemed such an approachable sort."

Finally in the door, Clara wheeled Tommy into the parlour as directed and entered a room straight out of Dickens. There was a velveteen cover on every available surface, mostly in black or dark green, and fussy fringes edged them all. Knick-knacks littered the mantelpiece, sideboard, and book case. A heavily patterned Persian rug filled the floor space and fought for dominance in the room with the intricately decorated flock wallpaper. Clara thought she could be no more overwhelmed until she saw the parrot.

Perched on a tall stand beside a circular table the bird was pure white except for its crest which was a vivid yellow. It raised this crest at the new arrivals in a mildly threatening manner before saying.

"Hello Clara and Thomas Fitzgerald."

"Good lord!" Tommy started in amazement. "How did they teach it to do that?"

Clara looked at the parrot suspiciously but it offered no further conversation.

"You can take a seat," Mrs Greengage appeared behind them, trailed by an optimistic looking Mrs Wilton.

Clara's heart sank as she saw the plainly hopeful look on her client's face. She wanted to wring Mrs Greengage's neck for playing so cruelly on someone's grief and desperation, but she remembered Tommy's words and managed to keep silent as they took their places at the table.

Mrs Greengage took a chair and ruffled a veil strategically around her neck.

"This is Augustus," she motioned to the parrot. "He is a fifth century reincarnated druid priest."

"Is he?" Clara said, earning a sharp nudge from her brother.

"Augustus uses the powers of the ancients to channel spirits into me. He is a conduit to the afterlife and as such deserves a little respect, Miss Fitzgerald."

The slightly off-centre gaze of the medium pinned Clara and she felt oddly put out that her comment had been so astutely picked up.

"My normal sessions with Mrs Wilton involve communication

with her late husband, but as we have guests she has kindly offered to set her own needs aside so I may contact spirits connected to you, Miss Fitzgerald."

Clara glanced at Tommy uncomfortably.

"You must give me a moment to prepare," Mrs Greengage pulled her veil over her head so that it nearly entirely masked her face, then she rested her arms on the table, palms up, with her thumb and forefinger pinched together.

"Would everyone join hands and relax," she whispered from behind the veil.

Mrs. Wilton brandished her hand eagerly at Tommy who took it and, in turn, offered his hand to Clara. She had her hands tightly balled in her lap, but with everyone looking at her she reluctantly removed one and clasped Tommy's hand.

"Take deep breaths," Mrs Greengage commanded taking her own long, deep breath. "Clear your mind and think of the person you would like to contact."

Clara obeyed, but with chagrin, and when her mind was clear she filled it with thoughts of her cat, Roger, who had died when she was twelve. It was a petty act of defiance but it felt good.

Mrs Greengage was taking deeper and deeper breaths, her ample chest rising and falling with a rattling of the pearls about her neck. Tommy grimaced at Clara.

There... is... a man coming through," Mrs Greengage whispered in a strained tone.

"Is it Arthur?" Mrs Wilton asked excitedly.

"No," Mrs Greengage carried on in a singsong voice, "His name is..."

"Albert!" cried out the parrot.

Tommy gave Clara an apprehensive look, but she was busy glaring at the parrot, lips narrowed into a thin, blood-less, line.

"Does anyone know an Albert?" Mrs Greengage asked.

Mrs Wilton shook her head in disappointment. Tommy took a sidelong look at his sister and then said;

"My father's name was Albert."

Clara looked at him sharply, but he refused to acknowledge her. Mrs Greengage was speaking in a drowsy voice once more, her head dipping to her chest.

"Albert is a strong character, he came through very quickly. He is wearing a tweed suit and has a small moustache. Does that sound familiar?"

"Yes," Tommy admitted.

"He has a gold watch in his hand, he is pointing at it, trying to indicate the time maybe? No, the name, the name on the watch."

"Edwards and Sons," Tommy said softly.

"Yes, that's it. But he doesn't seem happy, he is trying to give me the watch. Is it lost, this watch?"

"No, not lost," Tommy said uncomfortably. "Shut in a drawer, that's all."

"Ah, that explains it. He is showing me the watch and then putting it on. He wants you to wear it."

"Really?" Tommy gulped awkwardly.

"It will help, he thinks," Mrs Greengage drew a raspy breath. "Now he is looking for Clara. Clara, are you there?"

Mrs Wilton and Tommy both turned to Clara expectantly. She glared at them and kept her mouth firmly shut.

"She's here," Mrs Wilton answered for her.

"She doesn't like this does Clara, she thinks it is nonsense," Mrs Greengage's voice had taken on a child-like quality and now she teased out the words. "Clara, Clara, daddy's little girl, all grown up and with a mind of her own. A mind she is proud of, but what does daddy think of her running around playing detective?"

"Don't you dare!" Clara hissed though her teeth.

"Albert doesn't approve, hardly lady-like, is it? He wants you to give up the whole business, Clara."

Tommy held tightly to his sister's hand as she trembled with contained anger.

"You are putting words into my father's mouth," Clara said as calmly as she could manage.

"No dear, he is putting words into mine," Mrs Greengage seemed to be smiling beneath the veil. "Why can't you go get married Clara, like a good girl, he says? He only wants to see you settled. This business of yours will only end in heartache and for what? Chasing around for lost dogs and missing relatives? Albert is really unhappy."

"If you think I am fooled by these lies…" Clara began but Tommy pinched her hand and motioned to Mrs Wilton with his eyes.

"Albert is moving back," Mrs Greengage whispered, "back, back into the mists. Goodbye Albert. He sends his love to his dear children and now he is gone and the mist is clearing."

"Gone!" The parrot squawked merrily.

Mrs Greengage pulled back her veil and blinked her eyes as though coming out of a dream.

"Did Arthur come through?" She asked innocently.

"No," sighed Mrs Wilton, "and I was so hoping to be able to speak to him about paying the greengrocer."

Tommy stared at her mystified, but was then distracted by Clara standing.

"There are refreshments," Mrs Greengage waved at a side table. "First time guests often find a sherry necessary."

"I am not staying, thank you," Clara was pulling on her gloves as fast as she could.

"Clara!" Tommy hissed at her. "Remember what you are here for!"

Clara paused with one glove on and visibly composed herself.

"Perhaps a small sherry," she said with difficulty.

Mrs Greengage sprang up and started organising drinks. Stiffly Clara returned to her seat.

"Interesting, wasn't it?" Mrs Wilton whispered across the table.

"Enlightening," Clara said dryly.

"Fancy your father coming through first time," Mrs Wilton continued. "That is pretty special."

"It was a little frightening," Tommy conceded.

"Don't be afraid," Mrs Greengage had returned with the drinks. "It is like talking to someone on these new telephones."

"Except the caller is dead," Tommy said bluntly. "And this thing about the watch?"

"Spirits are just people and they have their own desires and wishes. Your father wants only the best for you."

"How long have you been a clairvoyant?" Clara interjected, but Tommy was relieved to see that she looked calm and ready to unravel this puzzle.

"Since I was a child, " Mrs Greengage said slowly and with a slight hint of hesitancy. "I inherited the gift from my grandmother, she was descended from a Romany family."

"Did she conduct séances?" Clara asked without a hint of malice.

Mrs Greengage took several moments to answer.

"It was not the 'done thing' in her day," she finally replied.

"Come, come, Spiritualism is not exactly new," Clara persisted.

"Some people view the power to speak to the dead as a little unsettling. My grandmother preferred to keep things private."

"And now?"

"Now?"

"You hold séances."

Mrs Greengage paused.

"Times are changing," she said darkly.

Tommy sipped his sherry with a frown and watched his sister out of the corner of his eye. He wasn't sure what to make of the whole event; the news about the watch had unsettled him. How could anyone know about that except for himself and Clara?

"Have you any more questions?" Mrs Greengage asked directly to Clara.

"Only one. Is it common for spirits to come through with riddles instead of clear messages?"

Mrs Greengage looked perplexed for a minute and then her eyes fell on Mrs Wilton and she grasped Clara's point.

"Not common, no. But everyone is different whether they are dead or alive."

Just then the parrot gave a strangled cry and fell from its perch with a thud to the floor.

"Augustus?" Mrs Greengage said, anxiously reaching out for the bird.

"Dead drunk," Tommy whispered in Clara's ear, motioning at Mrs Greengage's sherry glass. "He was helping himself."

"Augustus?" Mrs Greengage had the parrot in her hands and was shaking him gently.

"Oh dear, should we consult a vet?" Mrs Wilton fluttered.

The medium now had her ear to the bird's chest. Augustus' head hung back limply, a thin grey tongue protruded from his beak.

"He's dead!" Mrs Greengage wailed.

"Let me see," Tommy reached out for the bird which was handed over by the distraught clairvoyant.

Tommy gently splayed out one of the bird's wings and felt down between the edge of the feathers and the ribcage for a heartbeat. The room fell silent as everyone awaited the verdict. After failing to find a heartbeat Tommy felt the bird's tongue, which was cold and dry. He spent a few more moments looking for any sign of life, then shook his head morosely at Mrs Greengage.

The medium burst into floods of tears and Clara overcame her previous feelings to reach gently forward and clasp one of her hands.

"These things happen," she soothed.

"Oh dear," Mrs Wilton looked uncomfortably from one person to the next. "Oh dear."

Tommy carefully laid the dead parrot in the centre of the table, its wings neatly folded close to its sides.

"I'm terribly sorry," he said.

"He was in his prime," Mrs Greengage sobbed. "I bought him before the war. He lived through the German bombardment, even if the stress did cause him to lose most of his feathers. He had just finished growing them all back!"

There was a timid knock on the door.

"Go away Ernie!" Mrs Greengage snapped.

But the door opened anyway and a little balding man with a moustache crept in.

"I heard the noise," he said softly. "What has happened?"

"Augustus is dead!" Mrs Greengage wept.

The man called Ernie shuffled around the table and patted the fraught clairvoyant lightly on the back.

"There, there," he said absently.

"There, there!" Mimicked Mrs Greengage angrily. "Did you not understand? Augustus is dead!"

"Yes, yes... of course, dear," Ernie looked anxiously at the guests.

"I think this is Mr Greengage," Clara whispered to her brother. "Perhaps it is time we excused ourselves."

"Definitely," said Tommy.

Clara rose from her seat and coughed politely into her hand.

"Perhaps we had best be going?" She suggested.

Ernie nodded.

"Yes, perhaps that would be best."

With a flummoxed Mrs Wilton following them, the Fitzgeralds left the hubbub of the terrace house and stepped out into the relative calm of the night.

"Well I never," Mrs Wilton said as she stood on the garden path and looked back at the house. "Do you suppose the spirits took him?"

"Beg your pardon?" Said Clara.

"Spirits! They can be a dangerous business, they can draw the very life-force of a medium."

"Yes, I read about that in one of those books I got from the library. It was top of the list on warnings," Tommy added.

"Honestly!" Clara scowled at the pair of them. "What nonsense! Birds die all the time. Our great aunt was forever buying new canaries because the last one had popped its clogs only after a month or so of singing in the sitting room."

"That's small birds," Mrs Wilton protested. "Big birds like parrots can last for decades."

"Even so, more likely the bird died of natural causes, such as too much sherry, than 'spirits'," Clara insisted.

"I still don't like it," Mrs Wilton shuddered.

"It's getting cold to stand here and discuss this," Clara decided it was time to get away from séances and dead birds. "We best be on our way home."

"But you haven't said if you will pursue my case," Mrs Wilton said hastily.

The last thing Clara wanted to do just then was to start explaining her reasons for retreating from this case as fast as she could, while standing freezing to death on a doorstep.

"Perhaps you would call at my office tomorrow, Mrs Wilton, and we will discuss it," Clara said. "Any time will do."

"Oh. Very well." Mrs Wilton seemed a touch annoyed, but Clara couldn't face a debate on the matter there and then.

"I must get Tommy home out of the cold," she excused herself and pushed her brother's wheelchair out of the front garden and along the path as fast as she dared.

"You are going to turn her away aren't you?" Tommy asked dismally.

"Mrs Greengage is a fraud, therefore the riddles are frauds too."

"How did she know about the watch?"

Clara hesitated.

"I don't know, but if you believe that was genuine do you also think father wants me to give up my work as she said?"

Tommy scratched at his head and sighed.

"No, of course I don't believe that. It was just odd about the watch, that's all."

"And there's enough oddness in this world without Mrs Greengage adding to it," Clara pushed him up to their front door and it was quite clear the matter was settled.

"Shame," Tommy muttered to himself.

Chapter Five

Clara arranged logs in the hearth of the old brick fireplace in her office. The room was freezing and icicles had formed on the inside of the window. Donning her gloves she broke each one off and tossed them out of the window to the pavement below. The world was in the tight grip of winter, snow was thick on the roads and the workmen's carts were struggling to get through. Clara wondered what insanity brought her to work on a day like this. If she hadn't promised to see Mrs Wilton that morning she would have been tempted to stay at home.

She hadn't slept well, her mind had been on the obscure messages Mrs Greengage had given them from their father. Tommy had been rummaging through drawers first thing to find father's watch and was now proudly wearing it. That only made Clara think of the harsh words directed at her. Had it really been her father telling her to give up work or just the malice of Mrs Greengage? Her rational side firmly said the latter, but somewhere deep down there was this worm of worry making her second guess herself. It didn't help being in the cold office with no work to do except turn down Mrs Wilton's case when she arrived.

Picking up an old magazine she glumly thumbed through the pages to the fashion section. The black and white pictures brought back the times when she would have delighted in going shopping with her mother. Now all the coats and hats made her feel depressed, not least because she knew she could not afford most of them.

That was why she worked. Oh her father's investments kept the house going, paid the bills, made sure there was food on the table, but there was nothing left over for luxuries and these days that even meant a new warm coat. Clara threw the magazine aside angrily and picked out an old book on criminal psychology from the bookcase. It was from her father's library and had a fascinating section on phrenology. It was a load of nonsense, of course, but it teased the wistful side of Clara's nature to imagine that the solving of a crime could be just as simple as finding the right man with the right bumps on his head.

She read until the clock chimed midday. Rubbing her tired eyes she wondered where Mrs Wilton could be. Perhaps she had decided to give up trying to persuade Clara to help. She had been pretty obvious the night before about her feelings on Spiritualism.

Clara rummaged in her bag for the cheese sandwich Annie had made her that morning. The bread was stale and the cheese as hard as marble, but any food was welcome on a cold day. She was just working through the thick crust when her doorbell rang.

"Mrs Wilton, at last!" Clara said with relief, thinking she could at least get home as soon as she had dealt with the woman.

She hurried down the stairs and opened the door to a man in a dark overcoat.

"Oh," Clara said, noting to her horror that there was a uniformed policeman standing behind the stranger.

"Mrs Fitzgerald?" The man in the overcoat asked.

"Miss," Clara corrected automatically as she shook the hand he offered.

"Inspector Park-Coombs, miss. May I come in?"

"Of course," Clara stepped back from the entrance even more baffled and worried than before and showed the inspector the way upstairs.

"Has something happened?" She asked, thinking instantly of Tommy.

How often had she worried in her darkest moments about him doing something foolish?

"We don't really investigate things that haven't happened," Inspector Park-Coombs said glibly. "I believe you know a Mrs Greengage?"

Clara's stomach flipped over. Had the police discovered Mrs Greengage was a fraud and thought Clara was somehow working with her because of Mrs Wilton?

"I only met her last night," she said.

"You went to one of her séances?"

"Yes, under protest I might add."

"You don't believe in such stuff?"

"No, not really. The most exciting part of the evening was when the parrot fell off its perch."

"Parrot? What parrot?"

"Augustus," Clara said uncomfortably. "He had a heart attack or something and fell down dead."

"Ah, well now he can be reunited with his mistress," the inspector shrugged.

"What do you mean?" Clara spared an anxious glance for the policeman hovering in the office doorway.

"Mrs Greengage was murdered last night."

Clara was stunned into silence.

"Appears she was shot," the inspector continued. "What time did you leave her house?"

Clara took a moment to register the question and even then she could not formulate an answer.

"Murdered?"

"Yes. So what time were you there?"

Clara mentally shook herself.

"We got there just before seven and left around nine. I really didn't look at a clock, so I can't be certain."

The inspector calmly took a notebook from his pocket and wrote laboriously for a few minutes. Clara found herself starting to fidget uncontrollably. She still couldn't believe her ears.

"Are you sure?" She finally broke out and asked.

The inspector gave her a questioning look.

"That she was murdered? Perhaps it was some sort of accident?" Clara heard the desperation in her tone.

"It's quite hard to shoot oneself accidentally square in the heart," the inspector replied. "Besides we found no gun. Someone took it away."

The inspector glanced around the small office, pausing on the portrait of Clara's father.

"You're the daughter of Professor Fitzgerald, I believe?"

Clara was thrown for a second.

"Yes."

"Our medical fellow down at the station is always raving about him. Was one of his students before the war," the inspector paused thoughtfully. "Killed in London by one of those devices the Zeppelins dropped, wasn't he?"

"Yes, they were on a visit there. No one expected such a thing to happen."

"The Hun is devious like that," the inspector tapped his pen on his lip. "Tragic loss. Do you have other family?"

"Yes, a brother."

"He must have served in the war then?"

Now the pen tapped idly on the edge of the notebook.

"He did, yes."

"Did he keep his gun?"

The question, shot out of the blue, took Clara by surprise. She realised she had been happily allowing the inspector to lull her into a false sense of security which he had then equally deftly destroyed in an instant.

"I believe he did. A lot of the lads liked to keep mementos."

"And where does he keep it?"

"How should I know?" Clara snapped more than she had intended, she didn't want him to know how much he had unsettled her. "If you are implying Tommy might have shot Mrs Greengage then you are completely wrong. Tommy is confined to a wheelchair, he lost the use of his legs in No Man's Land when he was machine gunned. He couldn't stand long enough to shoot an empty bottle off a shelf, let alone a person."

"People usually tell me, when I accuse their loved ones, that they could never shoot a person because it is not in their nature. You on the other hand give me practical objections," the inspector smiled. Clara was beginning to distinctly dislike him.

"I wouldn't insult your intelligence," she said coldly. "Tommy served for years in the trenches. Of course I know he is capable in a dire situation of shooting someone. You would not believe me if I said otherwise and then anything else I said would be suspect."

"Very clever Miss Fitzgerald, but you miss my point, anyone in your household might have used that gun. You were one of the last four people to see Mrs Greengage alive," the inspector smirked.

"What about the husband?" Clara was determined not to be pinned to a murder no matter what the inspector said.

"Claims to have taken a sleeping draught that would have knocked him out for hours. Besides he doesn't have a motive."

"And I do?" Clara said astounded.

"I have it from a reliable source you considered Mrs Greengage a fraud who was preying on the naïve."

"Who said that?"

"Confidentiality, miss. I am also informed you became quite angry last night over some of the information Mrs Greengage gave you."

Clara was stunned. It seemed the whole world was ganging up on her just because she had a conscience.

"Mrs Greengage said some things to me that were spiteful, but I don't go around shooting people because they say hurtful things," Clara was flushing with embarrassed anger. "Being spoken harshly to is no motive for murder."

"Oh, but it can be," Inspector Park-Coombs said with a glint in his eye. "Many a maid has dropped a little poison into her mistress' tea because of a cross word."

"Well I am not a maid," Clara said sourly. "And I think you are grasping at straws Inspector. You are at a loss, so you are shaking a few trees to see if any rotten apples fall out."

"As I said before miss," the inspector grinned, "you are very clever. I'll pop round this evening to speak to your brother, miss. I am sure you would like to be there, being so protective and all."

The inspector tipped his hat at her and let himself out of the office and down the stairs. Clara followed and shut the door firmly behind him and the silent uniformed policeman who shadowed him.

Chapter Six

"Horrible man," Clara groaned, flopping down on the bottom stair and holding her head in her hands. "How dare he?"

She had barely been there a moment when there was a rap on the door. She didn't move. Had the inspector come back? The knock came again, more frantic this time. Clara stared at the door.

"Who is it?" She called reluctantly.

"Mrs Wilton, dear. Please let me in."

Thinking the morning could not get worse, Clara stood and opened the door. Mrs Wilton was shivering on the doorstep.

"I've been waiting for that ghastly inspector to leave. I'm frozen to the bone," she said.

"It's not much better in here," Clara stood back and let her through. "How did you know that was the inspector?"

"He visited me this morning," Mrs Wilton suddenly looked close to tears. "Isn't it awful!"

"Yes, very sad," Clara ushered her up the stairs.

"I mean, who will get in touch with Arthur for me now?"

Clara hid a scowl as she showed Mrs Wilton to a chair placed before the fire to catch its rudimentary warmth.

"Perhaps concerns about the more recent dead should be our top priority," Clara said as politely as she could manage.

"Oh dear, oh dear. Yes you are quite right. This whole matter has quite upset me and I have no one to talk to about it," Mrs Wilton let out a slight sob and fussed in her pockets for a handkerchief.

Clara leaned against the edge of her desk and tactfully looked askance as Mrs Wilton wiped her eyes.

"Who could have done such a thing?" Mrs Wilton said.

"I really don't know," Clara shook her head. "You knew Mrs Greengage better than me. Did she have a grievance with anyone?"

"Grievance? You mean someone she argued with or upset?"

"Precisely, after all she was in a profession fraught with controversy. Maybe she told someone something they didn't want to hear."

"She never spoke about other people and the Spiritualist Church members were full of praise for her."

Clara glanced out the icy window. It would be a frozen, cold funeral for Mrs Greengage.

"Well I suppose that means the inspector has only four suspects. Myself, you, Tommy and Mr Greengage."

"You mean the man who burst in last night? First time I had seen him," Mrs Wilton paused. "I must apologise to you Miss Fitzgerald."

Clara looked over.

"Whatever for?"

Mrs Wilton twisted the handkerchief in her lap.

"I did something rather awful and I fear you will be very upset and find it hard to forgive me."

Clara said nothing waiting for her to finish.

"When that inspector came this morning he gave me a fright with all his questions and I got in such a dither, and then it seemed as if he was accusing me of killing her!" Mrs Wilton directed an expression of disbelief at Clara. "Apparently Mrs Greengage had something of a reputation with the police. Some story about her predicting a murder and reporting it to the police, I think. Quite extraordinary."

"I should say so," Clara concurred, knowing Mrs Wilton's confessions tended to be on the long-winded side.

"Apparently after that the police took an interest in her work and even started compiling evidence that she was a fraud! Well what it all comes down to really, is that I was technically the last person to leave Mrs Greengage's. You were already walking away before I had quite got myself together and so that means you can't be my alibi, because I 'might' have hung around to commit the foul act," for a moment Mrs Wilton sounded hurt. "And there is no one at my house to say what time I came in. The police are suggesting I learned that I had been taken in by a fraud who had stolen the last of my money and out of desperation or revenge I took my dear Arthur's service pistol and shot the woman!"

"They are clutching at straws," Clara repeated.

"But that awful Mr Greengage told them I had hired you and lied and said it was because I thought his wife was a fraud, when I had quite clearly told Mrs Greengage you were there to help me with the riddles my husband had sent me!" Mrs Wilton snuffled again and dabbed at her eyes.

"They can't prove anything Mrs Wilton. It is all a load of nonsense."

"But it hurts to know that someone could even think that about one, even if it is only a policeman."

"They have suspicious minds," Clara responded soothingly.

Mrs Wilton fixed her eyes on the floor.

"But, you see, it made me terribly upset and... and that was when I thought, 'how dare they, when I was the one who believed in Mrs Greengage completely.' Then I thought how you had so clearly disliked her and I was angry because I thought you had already decided to turn my case down when I so badly needed help and... well... I just blurted out how they should be speaking with you rather than me after the things that Mrs Greengage said which obviously upset you," Mrs Wilton was breathless she had talked so fast, but she wasn't done yet. "I fear I sent them to your door and it was spiteful and unchristian and as soon as the Inspector had gone I felt bad and came rushing here to warn you, but I was too late."

"Never mind, Mrs Wilton," Clara said, finding herself feeling surprisingly generous over the matter. "As you said, Mr Greengage had already mentioned my name, so they were bound to come here eventually."

"You forgive me then?"

"Absolutely."

Mrs Wilton visibly sagged with relief. Then she looked up at Clara with a new expression of determination on her face.

"What are we going to do then?"

"Is there anything to do?" Clara asked puzzled.

"Of course! We are prime suspects to the police, if we don't do something to clear our names that inspector will trawl through our lives, raking out all our secrets, however mundane, until he can make a case against us."

"He has no evidence. He really can't do anything," Clara felt sorry for the frightened woman, knowing that at least she had Tommy and Annie as witnesses to her being home all night, but Mrs Wilton had no one.

"Even if he can't prove anything criminal the local scandal he will create will be bad enough. Do you think anyone will ask you to work for them after your name has been connected with a murder?"

Clara hesitated.

"That hadn't occurred to me."

"Yet it's true. Three years ago Mr Parson the banker was suspected of embezzlement, he was cleared but the missing money and the real culprit were never found and no one would use his bank anymore. He had to move away."

"That was during the war though, many crimes went unsolved," Clara remembered Mr Parson uncomfortably. She too had avoided his bank after the scandal, never thinking of the effect it might have.

"Mud sticks," Mrs Wilton said firmly. "And that inspector has his eyes set on us. You're a private detective, Miss Fitzgerald, go ahead and detect who did this."

"I'm not a policeman," Clara argued.

"All the better. Male private detectives do this sort of work all the time."

Clara noted the barbed implication.

"I can't interfere in police matters."

"Can't or won't?" Mrs Wilton stared at Clara fiercely. "This is serious, Miss Fitzgerald, and I don't think you realise that. Someone will be accused of this crime, the police have a lot on their hands, as you say many crimes went unsolved during the war and now the police are trying to crack down and prove themselves. I think that inspector has a bee in his bonnet about us."

"That I can't deny," Clara grumbled. "He did seem rather eager to make suppositions about the case. I suppose it would be sensible to explore the situation myself."

"Good. Good!" Mrs Wilton relaxed a little. "I am sure you will have this worked out in no time, I don't care what others say, women have a first rate mind for detection and I would not want to entrust my problems to a male detective, oh no!"

Clara decided not to remind her of their first meeting when Mrs

Wilton had been convinced she was going to speak with *Mr* Fitzgerald.

"I will do my best for both our sakes," she promised instead.

"That is excellent!"

Clara waited politely but Mrs Wilton seemed in no hurry to leave. There was an awkward silence which, in the end, Clara felt she had to break.

"Was there something else?"

"Now you mention it... there was one matter."

Clara inwardly groaned.

"And that was?"

"My riddles. Mrs Greengage never gave me the last ones but I thought she might have noted them down or told her husband. The spirits can communicate at any time and I am certain my Arthur would have had the foresight to ensure his messages were passed on before Mrs Greengage was so... so cruelly taken from us."

Clara had to let this sink in for a moment.

"Mrs Wilton..."

"I know you think it is a load of tosh, just like those policemen," Mrs Wilton snapped, "but I believe Mrs Greengage could speak to the dead and I *am* your client."

Clara held her tongue in case she blurted out that, as yet, Mrs Wilton was far from a client.

"It may be awkward," she said instead.

"All I am saying is ask the husband. I have no reason to go see him, but while you are investigating the murder you do. If I can't find my husband's money what will I do?"

There was a sudden fragile tremor in Mrs Wilton's voice and Clara kicked herself for failing to remember how desperate the woman was.

"I shall see what I can do," she agreed at last, "but you have to allow me my scepticism, it is what makes me a good detective."

She gave a mischievous smile.

"Of course!" Mrs Wilton smiled too. "I knew you were the right person for solving this problem the day I found your advert in the paper."

"I'll get on to the problem and update you when I can."

"Thank goodness, no rush though, but do hurry. I best head home now," Mrs Wilton stood and offered her hand to shake. "I am so glad I met you."

Clara escorted her to the door and watched her march off into the snow. It was only after she had gone Clara realised they had not discussed fees.

"Oh bother!"

Chapter Seven

There was a surprising lack of activity outside Mrs Greengage's house as Clara approached. The majority of the police had apparently already left, leaving behind one lone constable to guard the house. However, it was a cold day and the housewife two doors down had taken pity on him blowing into his frozen fingers and asked him in for a cup of tea. So there was no one outside the property as Clara hastened down the path and let herself in the front door.

Mrs Greengage's home was as she remembered, though in the stark light of day the wallpaper looked old and faded, the rug was filthy and the brass door furniture had not been polished in years. It seemed the clairvoyant was not the house-proud type.

Clara paused in the hallway. Her stomach was churning with a mixture of nerves and dread. She had no idea how she would react to the sight of blood or being in a room where a cold-blooded murder had been committed. During the war she had done a little nursing, but had found herself sent home more than once for fainting at the sight of blood. It didn't happen all the time, she could dress the most horrid wounds without flinching, then a person would appear with a sliced finger and she would take one look and pass out. It was very embarrassing and she tried her hardest to overcome the problem. Some of her fellow nurses had laughed at her, a few had scornfully called her feeble and weak. Clara knew she was neither, in an emergency she could hold herself together perfectly well, it was just that sometimes the sight of a person's blood made her go peculiar.

Now she stood in Mrs Greengage's hallway and wondered if she had the nerve to go on.

"Hello."

Clara jumped out of her skin at the friendly, unexpected, voice. Ahead of her, having just come from the kitchen, stood a young man in shirt-sleeves, drying a round circle of glass with a cloth.

"Did the constable let you in?" He asked.

"Yes," Clara lied quickly. "I am here on behalf of my client."

"Client?"

"Yes, I am a private detective."

"Oh, I didn't know women did that," the young man had an irritating smile on his face and Clara gritted her teeth.

"Women do many things these days, we are living in a new century, you know."

"I didn't mean to offend," grinned the young man, striding forwards to offer his hand to her, "Oliver Bankes, at your service. Or, am I not allowed to say that these days?"

Clara took Oliver's hand for politeness sake, wanting rather to slap him. He was around Tommy's age, with dark, slicked-back, hair and hazel-brown eyes. He held her hand a little longer than she liked.

"Clara Fitzgerald," she said. "You're not a policeman."

"Quite right," Oliver held up the glass disc. "I'm the photographer."

"Hardly the day for Mrs Greengage to be having her portrait taken."

"Police photographer," Oliver corrected. "I take pictures of crime scenes."

"Why?" Clara was utterly aghast.

"Nothing ghoulish," Oliver laughed. "For evidence, see sometimes a thing that doesn't seem important at first becomes really important later, but by then the crime scene may have been cleaned up or altered so the police use photographs. Besides it helps them remember where the body was. I thought you would know that being a detective?"

Clara bristled.

"I do not normally investigate murders," she said rather haughtily.

"Ah, more an errant husband and cheating at the Bridge club type business then?"

"No!" Clara said appalled. "I investigate real cases, proper crimes, just normally without dead bodies present."

"So why are you here?" Oliver asked simply.

"My client is a suspect in this case," Clara said uncomfortably. "She didn't do it of course."

"Of course!" Oliver agreed with only mild sarcasm.

"Anyway I am here to find evidence of the real killer."

"Can't the police do that?"

"They have been blinded by assumptions," Clara snapped, her patience running out with the infuriating photographer who was still grinning at her like a Cheshire Cat.

"You best see the crime scene then," Oliver held out his arm in a polite gesture to usher her through to the parlour. "My lens was a bit smeared from this morning, so I was giving it a wash. It always seems to go like that when I have been photographing babies."

"Someone killed a baby?" Clara gasped, her mind conjuring up a series of horrible images of tiny bodies.

"No, no!" Oliver said hastily. "Real babies, I mean living ones. I run the photography shop in the high street. Here."

He gave her a thin piece of cream card with his name and business address stamped on it.

"The police photography is only a side line. There really aren't that many murders in Brighton."

"Glad to hear it," Clara shoved the card into her handbag, determined to file it as evidence, or something, once she reached home.

"I don't want you to think I am morbid or anything," Oliver looked slightly abashed. "It can sound odd when you say you photograph dead people."

"Really?" It was Clara's turn to sound sarcastic.

"Look, go on in, I left my lens clip in the kitchen. I will only be a moment," Oliver vanished leaving Clara by the parlour door.

With a long deep breath, her stomach doing tiny somersaults, she opened the door and stepped inside.

The room had not changed since the night before. The sherry was still on the side, one glass still full. There was a faint scent of roses in the air and the table was laid with cards arranged in a half played game of patience. A single white feather lay among them.

What had Clara expected? Her eyes roved around the room and a guilty pang hit her. What was a clue and what wasn't? She could be looking at the vital piece of evidence to catch the killer and not know it. It was incredibly frustrating and she felt completely out of her depth.

Gingerly she edged around the table, looking at the cards as though they would shriek out some meaning to her. Was Mrs Greengage playing alone or with someone? Clara liked the question even if she had no answer, it sounded like something a real detective would think.

She edged a little further around the table trying to keep her eyes off the floor until she had fully screwed herself up for the sight of blood. She would not faint! She told herself sternly, especially not in front of Oliver. Mind over matter, she insisted inside her head, just think of it as spilt red ink. She shoved down all her fears, slammed them behind some mental door where they couldn't disturb her and told herself she was stronger than her hysteria.

And then her foot caught on something and she looked down.

Oliver came back in the room as Clara was biting down on the scream welling in her throat. She stood rigid and could almost feel the warmth draining from her face.

"I say, are you all right?" Oliver took her arm gently. "You've gone ever so pale. I should have warned you we hadn't moved the body yet."

Somehow he manoeuvred her into a chair even though she had gone stiff with shock.

"Would you like a drink of water?" He asked.

Clara shook her head, she didn't think she could swallow without gagging. The body of Mrs Greengage lay sprawled out at her feet. The clairvoyant's face was a horrid grey colour, her eyes were wide-open and staring at the ceiling. There was a fiery red hole in her chest.

She was wearing slippers. Clara found herself fixating on that one detail, perhaps because it was easier than trying to consider the whole dead body, or perhaps because they were what she had caught her foot on.

"I should have warned you," Oliver repeated apologetically.

"It is perfectly all right," Clara managed to find her voice. "I should have expected it."

"Your first body?" Oliver asked.

"I saw the odd one in the war," Clara admitted, "but not like this. Someone lying dead in a hospital bed is very different to this."

"Well you are doing grand. My first body, I couldn't stop shaking for an hour after seeing it and quite a few of the young PCs have been quite ill when they see their first."

"I don't intend being ill," Clara said firmly.

"Jolly good. So what do you want to do now? I could ask the constable to escort you home?"

"No!" Clara said hastily. "No, I have a job to do and a little fright won't stop me."

"Good for you," Oliver patted her awkwardly on the shoulder.

"Could you stop saying that, you sound like my old P.E. teacher."

"Oh," Oliver looked uncertain. "Shall I just get on with what I was doing then?"

"Please do."

Clara drew in a deep breath as Oliver set about arranging his camera tripod and re-installing the cleaned lens. She found she was irresistibly, and inexplicably, drawn to studying Mrs Greengage's corpse. The clairvoyant had removed her jewellery and her black shawl and seemed to have been in the process of preparing herself for bed.

"She wasn't expecting another visitor," Clara said suddenly.

"You think so?" Oliver asked as he rearranged his flash powder.

"You don't wait up for a guest half ready for bed," Clara cast her eye around the room. "There is a dressing gown on the armchair."

"So she didn't expect her killer," Oliver shrugged. "Is that important?"

"I don't know. But it does mean whoever did it came some time after the séance. Time enough for Mrs Greengage to start to get ready to go to bed."

"Mind your eyes," Oliver announced as he let off the flash and the room lit up brilliantly for a second.

"What do the police think?" Clara asked as she rubbed her eyes and the room came back into focus.

"You think they tell me anything?" Oliver laughed. "I just do the photographs. Most of the detectives think I am no better than the boys who clean out the police stables!"

"Really?" Clara was genuinely surprised.

"Most of them don't understand the concept," Oliver sighed. "Don't get me wrong, some do. Inspector Park-Coombs is a sharp spark, though he likes to pretend he is as dense as the rest of them."

Clara tried to hide her discomfort as he mentioned that dreaded name.

"Perhaps I have learned all I can here," she could think of nothing else but getting out of the room.

"Have you seen anything, a clue maybe, that will help your client?" Oliver asked.

"No, not really," Clara admitted, looking once more hopefully around the room. "Odd..."

"What is?"

"How after the shock has worn off you stop thinking about there being a dead body in the room. It is just, well, *there*."

"I know," Oliver was staring hard at her. "It is like being wrapped up in your own work so much you forget to notice that there is a pretty girl in the room."

Clara returned his stare evenly.

"I doubt you ever forget, Mr. Bankes," she said sharply.

Oliver grinned.

"If you want to see the pictures when they are done – to help your client, of course – come by my shop in a couple of days' time," he held out a card.

"You gave me one of those already."

"Oh yes, so I did," Oliver withdrew his hand hurriedly, flushing a little. "But do come by. I keep copies of every photo in case the police lose the originals, which happens more often than not."

"I shall bear it in mind," Clara replied. "Oh, I don't suppose you know where I can find Mr Greengage?"

"Across the road, at number 84." Oliver followed her into the hallway. "He needed somewhere to collect his thoughts."

"I don't blame him," Clara edged open the front door and tried to nonchalantly look outside and see if the constable was there.

"The constable didn't really give you permission to come in, did he?" Oliver said behind her.

She could tell from the manner of his voice he was grinning again.

"Good day Mr. Bankes," she said without looking back and then made a dash for the front gate.

She was just stepping through it as the constable emerged from two doors down. She let the gate swing to on its latch and crossed the road as though she had not just been sneaking around a dead woman's house. The constable was too concerned with his freezing fingers to give her much thought.

Chapter Eight

At number 84 Clara rang the bell and tried to think of a good reason to speak with Mr Greengage. A maid answered.

"Good afternoon, I was told Mr Greengage was here?"

The maid looked uncertain and, after indicating Clara should wait, hurried indoors. A few moments later a stern-looking woman appeared.

"Can I ask what is your business?" She said in a tone that matched her fierce appearance.

Clara braced herself.

"I'm from the Spiritualist Church. I take it you know Mrs Greengage was a member?"

The woman raised an eyebrow which Clara took as an acknowledgement that she did.

"I have come on behalf of Mrs Greengage's many friends as quickly as I could after hearing the news to see if her husband requires anything, specifically a temporary place to stay, but I see he has found himself a place here, so I shall just leave my condolences and go."

Clara turned away hoping she had judged the woman correctly.

"Wait."

Clara faced her again.

"As you may appreciate space and provisions are limited for a widow woman such as myself," the woman's stern appearance was sinking to one of consideration. "I am happy to offer Mr Greengage accommodation for a short stay – a very short stay – but as you say a burden shared is a burden lightened, and I see no reason why others shouldn't help out. After all, I hardly knew the Greengages."

"Not that he's a burden," she added quickly.

"I fully understand," Clara made herself appear as sympathetic as possible. "And I do find men in particular struggle to cope with circumstances such as these."

"Exactly! And they call us the weaker sex!" The woman clucked her tongue reproachfully. "Come in, won't you?"

The woman let her into a narrow, brown hallway. The maid was nearby and bobbed as she took Clara's coat.

"He is in the front parlour just there," the woman pointed to the nearest closed door. "I'll leave you in peace to talk with him."

Not bothering to make an introduction for Clara the woman disappeared down the hall with the maid and left her alone.

Clara gingerly opened the parlour door. Mr Greengage was sat in a high-backed armchair, hands resting on his knees limply and staring into the middle distance with a glazed expression. He was not a very big man, but looked even smaller huddled in the large chair.

Clara edged forward and he woke from his thoughts. He looked the sort of man to be easily dominated by such a forceful character as Mrs Greengage. His dark hair was greying at the sides and his round face seemed to mostly consist of a thick pair of round glasses.

"Can I help you?" He said in a sad tone, as though he was a tradesman and Clara had stumbled into his shop.

Suddenly Clara felt sick at the intrusion she was making on the man's grief.

"I'm terribly sorry about your wife," she said awkwardly.

"Were you a friend?"

Clara gulped, he clearly didn't recognise her from the night before, and now her throat felt tight as she formed a lie.

"Yes, from the Spiritualist Church."

"Not my cup of tea, all that," Mr Greengage stared thoughtfully at the parlour rug. "I've been an atheist since the war, but Martha believed whole-heartedly. I hope she found her Heaven."

"I'm sure she did," Clara sat herself down in a chair and tried to appear comfortable. "And she would be concerned to know you were all right, I'm sure."

"Oh, I'm fine." Mr Greengage grimaced. "Well not fine, obviously, but surviving."

"I can only imagine the shock of it all," Clara shook her head sadly. "Bad enough these people break into our homes, but to be prepared to kill as well…"

"I'm sorry, but what do you mean?" Mr Greengage had a frightened little smile on his face.

"Nothing really, I presumed she was shot by an intruder, a burglar perhaps."

"Nothing was stolen," Mr Greengage said bluntly. "No, they came for her."

Clara was no longer feigning when she fell into a stunned silence for a moment.

"You honestly believe it was a deliberate act, not an accident?"

Mr Greengage studied his hands as though he had only just noticed he had them.

"She had enemies."

"Surely not!"

"As sure as I am sitting here telling you she was purposefully murdered," Mr Greengage was sharp-tongued and then he softened again. "It was that business at Eastbourne. She took herself too seriously, that was all, that speaking to the dead nonsense, no offence madam."

"None taken, though I don't see how being a medium could make her hated enough for someone to want to kill her."

"She was convinced she was in touch with a woman who had been murdered," Mr Greengage snorted. "Kept me awake some nights she did going on and on about how her conscience would not let her rest until she told the police and me, being an even bigger fool, finally got sick of it all and told her to go to the damn police. I was convinced they would send her away with a flea in her ear and the matter would be resolved, but blow me, if they didn't actually believe her!"

"They arrested someone?"

"The case wasn't strong enough, but they certainly made a fuss and my dear Martha was at the centre of it all. She made an enemy that day, I tell you."

"Who?" Clara asked, hardly able to believe her ears or her luck.

Mr Greengage hesitated.

"Bumble, or something similar was his name. I kept out of it, anyway the case came to nothing and then this fellow starts talking of suing us for damages and there was no choice but to leave and come here."

Clara leaned back in her chair, her breath taken away by the story.

"But would this Bumble fellow really murder her?"

"Oh, I don't know!" Mr Greengage's voice suddenly broke with emotion and he cradled his head in his hands. "I should have been there, not asleep. I should have protected her."

Clara reached out and gently touched his arm.

"It couldn't be helped."

"It's these damn sleeping draughts I take," Mr Greengage curled his hands into fists angrily. "Ever since the war the nightmares have been terrible and without the powders I just get no rest."

"That isn't your fault," Clara said soothingly.

"I should have been awake!"

"And do you think the killer would have hesitated about killing you too?"

He paused.

"When someone has a gun and wants to kill it really doesn't seem to matter to them if they happen to take out one victim or two," Clara squeezed his arm. "It appears to me you had a lucky escape and in doing so maybe you can help the police catch the killer."

"How do you mean?"

"Well, you have to think, try and remember something useful about last night."

"I was asleep," Mr Greengage said miserably.

"Even in dreams normal events can manifest. Do you remember any detail of a dream that may be important?" Clara pressed on. "A sound? A noise that stood out?"

"No! No!" Mr Greengage clutched at his head again. "I don't remember a thing."

Clara inwardly sighed, they were at a dead end.

"Perhaps I should be going," there was no response from Greengage so she stood to leave.

"Oh, one last thing," she acted as though she had just remembered something important. "A woman approached me. Oh dear, what was her name? She was quite upset about your dear wife and kept babbling on about riddles. She was trying to track you down but I managed to dissuade her, she didn't seem quite the sort you would want descending on you at a time like this."

"That sounds like Mrs Wilton."

"Yes! That was the name – Wilton. She seemed a bit of a nuisance really."

"She is," Mr Greengage groaned. "My wife was in touch with Mrs Wilton's late husband and kept giving her these riddles, clues to the man's lost savings or something. I thought it was all hogwash."

"She did seem rather persistent, but what would she want with you?"

"Oh blast, I had forgotten. My wife was holding back some of the riddles. Even though she had them all she pretended she didn't," Mr Greengage had the decency to look abashed. "You have to understand, she was still trying to build up her clientele and money was tight. Mrs Wilton was a promising regular and she was trying to keep her as long as she could. I know it wasn't ethical."

Clara kept her expression pointedly neutral.

"That explains what Mrs Wilton was going on about. I imagine she will try and visit you."

"I couldn't stand that," he rubbed at his temples. "Perhaps... maybe... would you give the riddles to her? It would save me having to see her."

Clara made a pretence of looking mildly put out, then appeared to relent.

"I suppose so. I did come to offer any assistance I could."

"So kind," Mr Greengage mustered a smile as he stood. "They are back in the house. I will take you across."

"Will you be all right going back, I mean..."

"Yes. Yes," Mr Greengage brushed off the comment sharply. "The riddles are in my study anyway, and I intend going home as soon as I can. I don't like being out of the house for long."

Clara looked at him curiously, but as she had got what she wanted (or rather Mrs Wilton had) she decided to keep her peace.

Mr Greengage led the way across the road and addressed himself to the constable on duty. Within seconds they were in the house. Clara was relieved to see Oliver had gone, there was something about him that made her lose her entire sense of self-confidence when in his presence. Of course, she would have to visit him eventually if she wanted to see the photographs of the crime scene, more was the pity.

Mr Greengage led them past the shut door of the parlour where his wife still lay on the carpet going quietly cold, and into the room just behind it. The study was dominated by a writing desk and a large armchair pressed close against one wall.

"I kept the records," Mr Greengage said absently as he rifled through the desk. "Here you are."

He handed over an envelope thick with a small wad of papers. Clara gave them a glance and then turned to the forlorn widower.

"What will you do now?" She asked with genuine concern.

Mr Greengage shuffled about his room, picking up and putting down books and papers.

"I don't know really, I haven't worked since the war," he fiddled with a pen on the desk. "Martha kept us going. You see, after the war I found I didn't like being in open spaces too long."

Clara didn't understand, but merely nodded.

"Martha was helping me get my confidence back but I guess that is all gone now."

Clara suddenly felt so sorry for the pitiful figure before her that she wished she could do something for him.

"If you need anything you can always call me," Clara reached for her purse where she had some business cards and then stopped herself. If he saw the cards he would know she was a detective and her 'neighbourly love' approach would be ruined. Besides she didn't want him to think she had come only to ask questions, even if that was her reason.

"I'll write my phone number down for you," she pulled a piece of paper from the desk and scribbled her number down.

"Thank you," Mr Greengage said vaguely. "Now, if you don't mind, I would like to be here by myself for a while."

"Of course," Clara pushed the slip of paper towards him so he would see it and then let herself out of the study. As she walked down the hallway she heard him begin to sob softly.

Outside she said goodbye politely to the constable to avoid arousing suspicion and stepped onto the pavement. The evening was drawing in rapidly and Clara pulled her collar up against the cold. She hoped Annie had a hot meal cooking for her when she arrived home.

She was just reaching the end of the road when she noticed the footsteps behind her. There was nothing particularly odd about them, but the hair on the back of her neck stood on end at the sound.

She stopped at the curb. The footsteps stopped. She crossed the road and headed up another street and the footsteps followed. She stopped again, abruptly this time, and so did the footsteps. Now Clara was certain something odd was happening. She turned sharply and a few feet away the shadowy outline of a man could be seen just beyond the circle of light cast by a street lamp. As she stared at him he turned around and left.

Clara realised she was shaking. Her heart was pounding. She doubled her pace and headed for home as fast as she could.

Chapter Nine

A nnie noticed she was out of breath as she took her coat.

"Are you all right, Clara?"

Clara looked at the girl's pinched expression of concern and felt her fear slowly leave her.

"I'm fine Annie, I just rushed home," she said.

She had met Annie at the hospital during the war. Having lost both parents and her sister during an aerial bombardment Annie was an emotional wreck as she sat on a bed having glass pulled from her arms and legs.

There was something about her that struck Clara instantly. She didn't flinch as her wounds were treated, but as soon as she thought she was alone she sobbed her heart out. Annie never talked about her family and, to the doctors and nurses, she presented a cheery façade, a 'one-must-get-on-with-things' outlook that always hit Clara as being forced. Then one day, one of her other patients confided something to her that was troubling. Annie, in a dark moment, had confessed she was planning to kill herself as soon as she was released. She couldn't face going on alone, the future seemed just too daunting.

Clara made up her mind in that moment. Before Annie was due to be discharged she asked if she would be interested in working for her.

She made it sound as though Annie would be doing her a huge favour, and that was not entirely untrue. Tommy was due home and with his injuries Clara was dreading being in the house alone to cope. Oddly, as she spoke with Annie, she found herself confiding all this. She had not talked so openly to anyone else, but in retrospect it had been the right way to win over Annie. She was a naturally caring soul and the thought of being useful to someone gave her a purpose to cling to. Both women came together because of their terror of the unknown ahead.

Leaving Annie shaking her head, as she did not entirely believe what she had just been told, Clara went to find her brother in the drawing room.

"Good evening, sis," Tommy called from the table where he was surrounded by books.

"Have you heard the news?" Clara asked.

"About the late Mrs. Greengage? Yes, it's all about the town. Annie told me when she came home with the potatoes."

"I'm afraid I am on the suspect list."

"Really?"

"Yes, the Inspector says I could have done it with your old service pistol."

"You'd have a hard job," Tommy shrugged. "Had the thing with me in No Man's Land. It was half submerged in mud for ages before they found me and brought me back. The inside was full of the black stuff and I hardly had the inclination to clean the thing. Whole firing mechanism is jammed."

Clara sank into a chair.

"Well that is a relief!"

"Why? Did you think you might have done it in a walking trance and not remembered?" Tommy grinned.

"Don't be silly," Clara snorted.

"That just leaves Mrs Wilton then."

"She can't have done it," Clara hesitated, "Can she?"

"Doesn't seem the type."

"Is there a 'type'?"

Tommy thought for a moment then shrugged.

"Anyway, she was still rather keen on the riddles she thought her husband was sending by spiritual telegraph," mused Clara. "Had me go and collect the remaining ones, so she must still believe in Mrs Greengage."

"Doesn't mean she didn't kill her, if she thought she was being used," Tommy rubbed his chin. "Did you say there were more riddles?"

"Yes."

"Can I look?"

Clara fished the envelope out of her handbag and passed it to Tommy.

"She was definitely stringing Mrs Wilton along, you know."

"Right. But if Mrs Wilton killed her for taking her money unlawfully wouldn't she make sure she had all the riddles first?" Tommy thumbed open the envelope.

"I don't know, you were the one who suggested she might have a motive if she felt used," Clara screwed up her eyes, this whole nightmare was giving her a blistering headache.

"You have to test a theory, check out its flaws before you can consider it valid. It says so in this book I found written by an ex-Scotland Yard detective."

"Why is he an ex-detective?" Clara asked, opening one eye.

"Perhaps he wanted to pursue his career as a writer," Tommy answered sarcastically. "Hey, where did you get these riddles from?"

"Mr Greengage gave them to me out his desk."

"Well, I think Mrs Wilton isn't the only one being strung along. They are all just blank slips."

Clara sprung upright.

"Pardon?"

Tommy displayed the pieces of paper he had just removed from the envelope in his hands. They were all blank.

"Mr Greengage, I presume?"

"No, no," Clara took a piece of paper and stared at it. "He had no reason to. How would he know I would ask for the riddles? He had no time to prepare a dummy envelope and, anyway, what did he have to gain apart from the continued harassment of Mrs Wilton?"

Tommy had no answer.

"They are just riddles," Clara turned the paper over and over in the lamplight as if to try and reveal some secret. "If Mrs Greengage did not have any more of them why didn't he just say so?"

"Perhaps he didn't know. He thought his wife had written the rest but actually she hadn't."

"That makes no sense either," Clara looked at the papers forlornly. "I don't understand any of this."

Tommy was prevented from replying by a knock on the parlour door.

Annie appeared.

"There is a police inspector at the door says he must speak to you."

"Park-Coombs," Clara looked meaningfully at Tommy, but he just appeared puzzled. "Send him in, Annie."

The inspector seemed slightly more frazzled than he had that morning as he entered the room. Clara wondered if his enquiries were proving less fruitful than he had imagined.

"Miss Fitzgerald. Mr Fitzgerald."

"Inspector Park-Coombs, this is my brother Tommy," Clara introduced them. "Tommy, the Inspector thinks I am a cold-blooded murderer."

"Hazard of the job, miss," the inspector grimaced.

"Well, I think I can put your mind at rest Inspector, at least where Clara is concerned," Tommy announced, enjoying the moment of triumph. "You see, my service pistol is completely inoperable."

"I see," the Inspector said mildly.

"I'll fetch it if you like," Tommy started to push his wheelchair away from the table, but the inspector stopped him.

"I'll retrieve it, if you don't mind sir. Case of ensuring the evidence isn't tampered with. I'm sure you understand."

"I've been here all day, if I was going to break my own gun I would have done it by now."

"Indeed sir, but even so..."

Tommy waved away the rest of the words.

"All right Inspector, but I assure you I didn't fill the thing with mud from Flanders in the last half hour just to get my sister off the hook."

"Could you direct me to it?"

"My bedroom is down the hallway, last room on the right. Used to be the garden room. You'll find the pistol in the dresser, second drawer down under some vests. Annie could show you."

"No need," the inspector let himself out of the room and vanished.

Clara and Tommy sat in silence for a while, then she looked at her brother.

"Is it odd that though I feel relieved for myself I feel angry for Mrs Wilton?"

"Not at all," Tommy told her. "Quite natural."

"I wish I could help her more but I feel at a complete loss. I am out of my depth."

"Don't give in old thing, not now."

Clara sighed and dumped the blank riddle papers into the fireplace.

"Could Mrs Wilton have realised she was being defrauded before she involved me in this matter?" She pondered.

"If that was truly the case, why would she hire you?"

"I have to face the possibility that she may have considered my skills too inadequate to find the truth, thus she felt safe asking me to look into the crime, knowing that by doing so she would be covering up any motive for murder."

"You are being too hard on yourself," Tommy said sternly. "Besides, we have not even begun to consider the parrot."

Clara took a moment to register what he had said.

"The parrot?"

"Mrs Greengage's white cockatiel who popped his clogs the night of the séance."

"Augustus?"

"Yes. I've been looking up talking birds in father's old encyclopaedias," Tommy pulled a large, heavy book towards him.

"I thought poor Augustus died of a heart attack?" Clara said, still trying to catch up.

"He might have done, but Mrs Greengage was quite right in saying he was in his prime. By parrot terms he was still a young bird, which makes it seem all the more odd that he should drop dead the same night as his mistress."

"You are quite right Mr Fitzgerald," the inspector reappeared in the room. "I was equally perturbed and had our laboratory run a quick test on the bird. Early indications suggest Augustus died from a high dose of strychnine. Question remains how and why was it done?"

Clara felt the world was spinning away from her.

"Someone killed the parrot?"

"It may have been an accident. The drug was probably meant for his mistress, which means we are looking for a very determined killer who planned this crime carefully," the inspector placed Tommy's service pistol on the table. "As you said sir, completely unusable."

"Thank you, Inspector. Was there anything else?"

"No, I doubt I will need to disturb you again, I will take my leave," the inspector doffed his hat and left without waiting for Annie to show him out.

"I don't like it, Tommy," Clara said as soon as he was gone. "Does a poisoner suddenly decide to take up shooting to claim their victim? One method distances one from the crime, the other means the act has to be up close and personal. Why such a dramatic change?"

"Maybe they became desperate?"

"But the shooting seems so... so spur-of-the-moment. It just doesn't fit together right."

"There is another thing that doesn't make sense," Tommy frowned as he added to the confusion. "White cockatiels are mimes, they talk but only by repeating what they have heard and it takes ages to teach them phrases. Trainers work with these birds for months just to get them to say a few simple sentences. Yet Augustus was able to say peoples' names and recite messages instantly."

"Oh my!" Said Clara.

"Exactly! It shouldn't have been possible."

"Unless he was a very unique bird? But somehow I doubt that. He was a trick like everything else."

"So how does that help or hinder us?"

Clara shook her head.

"We have far too many unanswered questions and I have a pounding headache," Clara felt the pain spiking across the top of her head as she spoke. "I think I will go lay down for a while."

Chapter Ten

C lara lay on her bed, but it was hardly restful, not when her mind was whirring so fast. Strychnine and then a shooting? She didn't like it, it felt awkward. Poisoning was such a subtle approach compared to drawing a gun on someone, but was she trying too hard to see reason where there was none? In a story it would make no sense, but in real life things tended to be more messy. Murderers did random things, especially when a situation demanded urgency. Yet that left the question, what urgency? For that matter, why would anyone, aside from this mysterious Bumble character, who she wasn't convinced about, want to kill Mrs Greengage in the first place?

She tried to rack her brain for something she could compare the event to, but all that kept springing to mind were the stories she had heard of the Borgias in school. At the time her teachers had felt she had an unhealthy appetite for that long dead Italian dynasty, who were renowned for popping off unwanted relatives and rivals with poison. But her father had been less troubled and saw it as a promising natural curiosity. Though Clara doubted he had ever imagined she would be using that knowledge to try and solve a real murder.

Then again, perhaps all these thoughts of the Borgias that were stuck in her head were more of a nuisance than a help. Perhaps they were blinding her? They again made her feel the change of murder style was all wrong. Something made no sense. Perhaps if she could work out how the poison was administered?

Then there was that other nag. Wasn't poison the usual tool for women? Most poisoners were female, as the case of Lucrezia Borgia emphasised. It was a feminine weapon, but that left her suspicions firmly pointing again at Mrs Wilton – no one else had cause or convenience to commit the crime.

It was all such a jumble. Clara gave up trying to rest and went down to dinner.

Annie had just brought a gammon joint to the table as Clara arrived. Tommy was already at his customary place at the top of the table.

Annie smiled at the compliment before scurrying away again. She returned a moment later with a dish of slightly over-boiled sprouts.

"Last in the pantry," she announced not noticing Tommy's nose wrinkling in distaste. "I'll just get the potatoes."

"Really, sprouts again?" Tommy said.

"They are good for you," Annie reminded him.

"But I hate them," Tommy pulled a face.

"You are not a child who pulls a tantrum over their supper. You are a grown man who knows to eat his veg," Annie scolded him.

"Come on, old thing." Tommy turned his full smile on the girl. "Indulge a poor crock at his dinner time."

"You are not a crock, Tommy," Annie said with a spark of emotion that surprised Clara.

She was aware her brother had a soft spot for Annie, until that moment she had thought the infatuation very much one-sided.

Annie disappeared to return with the potatoes. It was noticeable that when she served the food, she only gave Tommy one Brussel sprout; a compromise on her part. The steady click of cutlery accentuated the silence and the throbbing in Clara's skull. Clara decided she better start the conversation.

"What have you two been up to today?"

"Well, I had hoped to return to the book shop but my nursemaid banned me," Tommy said with a mischievous glance at Annie.

"You complained of a sore throat yesterday and I wasn't going to be responsible for letting you catch pneumonia," Annie said piously, though a hint of a smile played on her lips.

"Ah, the ex-detective's book?"

"Good guess, Annie collected it for me."

"Yes, when I went for the gammon and quite an episode it was too," Annie suddenly became animated as she relayed her gossip. "That new maid from Mrs Pembroke's house was in there and making a fine fuss at not being able to get a map of Brighton for less than 5d."

"Still not found her feet in the town, I imagine," Tommy said.

"Most people just ask directions," Clara observed.

"She is a fine one," Annie tutted. "You would think she served the queen or some such person, the way she goes on and always turning her nose up as if Brighton isn't good enough for her."

"A maid buying a map, honestly! Mrs Pembroke can't have her running that far afield, surely?"

"And when she finally decided on paying the 5d the fuss she made because the maps she looked at didn't cover all the countryside and villages around the town as she wanted. I said to myself, she wants an atlas not a map, way she goes on."

Clara smiled as her mind relaxed and tuned into the everyday matters that didn't involve death which Annie relayed. Even the headache seemed to be lifting.

"Thick as thieves with that little Elaine as works for Mrs Wilton, she is. I had meant to say to you about it. Thought perhaps you could mention it to Mrs Wilton before that girl turns Elaine's head with all her talk about what she would do if she had a spare bit of money. Fancies herself a lady that one."

"See what I miss when I don't go out?" Tommy complained with a devilish smile.

"Tsk, Thomas Fitzgerald, I only think of your health," Annie pouted.

"And very glad I am for it too, but I get fed up being cooped indoors."

"Well the weather is about to turn and then you can be a gad-about again," said Annie, trying to press a disintegrating sprout onto her fork. "Or so the boy who works for Mr Bankes tells me."

"Mr Bankes?" Clara said sharply.

"The photographer in the high street. Bit experimental, or so I hear, very keen on 'natural light' apparently for his pictures, which is why he keeps such a close watch on the weather, so he can predict when to take the best portraits or something. So his errand boy says, I think its half nonsense the lad makes up, he reckons Mr. Bankes gets his forecasts from a man in London!"

The conversation reminded Clara of a job she had to do the next day which she wasn't looking forward to. Annie was clearing away the dinner plates and talking about pudding, but Clara protested her headache and said she was going to bed early.

Upstairs she lay in her dark room, her mind flicking from the happy noise of Annie and Tommy laughing downstairs to the visit she must pay to Bankes the next day and his crime scene photos.

Chapter Eleven

Bankes' photography shop stood between a baker's and a butcher's shop, which had created an oddly pleasing rhyme in Clara's head and made her wish Oliver had been a candlestick maker to fit in with his neighbours.

It was a neat, but not grand shop, painted dark green with the name picked out in gold and the window blocked with thick black drapes like an undertaker's. Instead of a display of coffins or memorial stones, Bankes had several large family group shots and portraits mounted on easels. A quick glance certainly would have given no notion of the darker side of Oliver's work.

Clara pushed open the heavy door and stood in a small reception area that smelt faintly of chemicals. There was a counter with a bell on it. She waited a moment, then rang it.

"Coming!" A harassed looking woman with her hair all at odds appeared from a side door. "Are you a client?"

"Not as such, but Mr. Bankes is expecting me."

"Can I take your name, dear?" The woman reached out for a scrap of paper with one hand and a pair of glasses with the other. "Memory like a sieve, so I write everything down. I blame working around these fumes all day. Right, who should I say is calling?"

"Miss Clara Fitzgerald."

"I'll tell him straight away, but he'll be a moment. The cat has knocked a load of bottles all over, yet again. Gone on the floor and on Mr Bankes, poor soul. Some of them chemicals can scald you know. But won't have a word said against that cat. Just wait here, won't you?"

The woman bustled off again and Clara took to surveying the many photographs lining the walls. Gentlemen stared out at her with their thick moustaches, and elegant ladies in heavy dresses scowled, while alongside them more modern artistic images of girls in cloche hats and shapeless dresses displayed the changing times and fashions.

"Some of those are my father's."

Clara jumped at the unexpected appearance of Oliver behind her and was instantly cross with herself.

"I thought some were a little before your time, unless you are much older than you look," she said.

"I'll treat that as a compliment," Oliver grinned, as Clara blushed with annoyance. "Father rented this place after the war, said the old studios held too many memories, but he prefers to do artistic photography these days and leaves the running of the business to me. Would you like to come through and have a cup of tea?"

Without waiting for a reply, the eager photographer led Clara through a curtained archway and into an untidy backroom that served as his office space. The walls were lined with heavy wooden filing cabinets and an old desk was wedged between two of them and littered with papers, loose photos, a week's worth of newspapers and a tea plate with the remains of cold toast sitting on it. The office had very much the feel of a man's working domain and that wasn't just because of the odd scattered hat or jacket, or the smell of tobacco. It was the sort of place women would rarely enter, Clara suspected, even perhaps the bumbling receptionist.

Oliver dragged a stack of unused photography plates from a green leather armchair and motioned for Clara to sit. He then proceeded to remove a well-fed tabby cat from his own wooden desk chair. The creature gave a disgruntled yawn and headed out of the door.

"Mrs Grimby, pot of tea please?" Oliver yelled before sitting at his desk with a smile. "So, to what do I owe the pleasure?"

Clara was regaining her sense of calm now she was sitting in the studio surrounded by the detritus of ordinary life.

"You invited me to come and see the photos you took at Mrs Greengage's house."

"So I did," Oliver nodded, the smile fading a little. "Are you sure you want to see them?"

"It can hardly be worse than seeing the actual dead body," Clara replied with false bravado.

"I suppose," Oliver got up and went to a filing cabinet. "Inspector Park-Coombs has had copies of course."

He brought back a selection of black and white pictures.

"I take lots in case some don't come out," Oliver was a bit apologetic about the number of photos. "Lighting outside the studio can be so tiresome."

Clara cast through the pile, scenes of Mrs Greengage's parlour from all angles and directions flitted before her eyes; close-ups of the table and rug, and the sideboard where glasses had been stacked.

"There is something missing," Clara tapped the pictures and looked meaningfully at Oliver. With a sigh he handed over the photographs he had carefully held back.

Clara looked at the new images displaying Mrs Greengage's body. Oliver had been as thorough with these as with the other shots and there were several taken from varying angles and distances.

"She doesn't look like a woman who was shot," Clara remarked, surprising herself with the statement.

"How do you mean?"

"She looks peaceful, maybe a little puzzled, but not scared or distressed."

"Most murder victims don't," Oliver answered. "It's a myth of fiction that people die with their faces twisted in an awful grimace, most just look, well, dead."

Clara sorted through the photos again, vaguely aware that she was no longer disturbed at the sight. This Mrs Greengage felt distant, removed, not a woman she had met and who had then been horribly murdered. Not a woman she had sat and drunk sherry with only two nights before.

Sherry!

She flicked back through the shots until she reached the one of the sideboard and drinks cabinet. There were all the glasses, all empty except for one. How many had had sherry that night? Herself, Tommy and Mrs Wilton, that would account for three glasses, but the fourth one had been for Mrs Greengage and she had never touched hers because of the commotion surrounding the sudden death of Augustus. And the poison found in the parrot had made them all assume that someone had wanted to kill Mrs Greengage, but had anyone thought to test the glass of sherry? It had to be in there, didn't it? Not the whole sherry bottle or else they would all be dead, but just that glass, specifically that glass.

"We have to test the sherry in that glass, Mr Bankes," she said aloud just as Mrs Grimby walked in with the tea tray.

"Miss Fitzgerald is a keen amateur photographer, Mrs Grimby," Oliver said, carelessly knocking some papers over the top of the Greengage photographs.

Mrs Grimby gave Clara a smile and left the tea tray on a stack of old photography magazines.

"She doesn't like the murder pictures," Oliver said when she was gone again. "Sorry, I should have mentioned that sooner. But what was that about the glass?"

"The police now know Augustus was poisoned and the natural conclusion that I jumped to when I was told was that the poison was actually meant for Mrs Greengage. The means was the bother, but I saw that picture and it was so obvious. It had to be in the sherry, but not the decanter, else we would all have perished, but just one glass. Specifically the full glass in this picture. Augustus drank from it. It was a shocking risk for the murderer to take, presumably he knew how the glasses were laid out and handed around so he could guess which glass would ultimately end up in Mrs Greengage's hand, but it still could have easily gone to someone else. Of course, this is assuming there *is* poison in that glass, the same poison that killed Augustus."

Oliver gave her a confused frown.

"You mean... this could point to the killer?"

"Yes... I mean... maybe. Actually, I am not sure, but it must mean something, I suppose. I shall have to see the Inspector straight away," Clara was gathering up her things without even touching her tea. Oliver tried to detain her.

"You're going now?"

"No time like the present."

"Perhaps there is more in the photographs? Perhaps another look?"

"No, I've seen enough. Thank you for helping me, Mr Bankes.

"Oliver, please. And if you need to see the photos again come straight here, I am almost always around."

They had made their way back to the reception area, and Clara was fumbling with her hat as she darted out the door.

"Thank you again, Oliver. Goodbye."

She waved as she dashed off.

"Bye," Oliver called after her.

He watched her run up the road, her hat half on and her hair flying wild. He was picturing her through a camera lens, capturing that moment of excitement and haste. Oliver wondered, as the door slowly closed, what it would be like to take a girl like Clara to the music hall.

Chapter Twelve

T he sergeant on the front desk of the police station couldn't have been less helpful if he had tried.

"You can't just waltz in and see the Inspector, it isn't procedure."

"But it is extremely urgent," insisted Clara.

"So are most things people come in here for," the sergeant replied with heavy sarcasm.

"He will want to see me," Clara demanded, but the sergeant had flipped open one of the big ledgers on his desk and was studiously ignoring her.

"Honestly!" Clara gasped in exasperation looking around the police station for inspiration. There was only an old drunk asleep on a wooden bench which didn't help her at all.

"It's about a murder," Clara hissed to the sergeant, but he didn't even look up. "How do you ever solve crimes if you never listen to anyone?"

"What crime is that, Miss Fitzgerald?"

Clara glanced up and was immediately torn between hope and annoyance at the face that greeted her. His name was Percy Boyle, an odious boy Clara had had the misfortune to go to school with. He had been a typical bully, though Clara was exempted from his more unpleasant torments because of having an older brother who was quite good with his fists. Tommy had sent Percy sprawling more than once.

The fact that Percy had made it into the police was more down to a shortage of men with all their limbs attached after the war than to any real talent on his part. He had been overlooked for military service due to a horrendous squint that made it seem as if he was always talking to a person's left shoulder. Getting into the police force had been a lucky break for him and maybe it was for her too. Percy might be an idiot, but his healthy respect for Tommy (thus transposed to his sister) might mean he could help her to see the inspector.

"I have vital information on a case for Inspector Park-Coombs, but the sergeant here won't let me through," she explained briefly to Percy.

"Not procedure," tutted the sergeant, irritated to feel the need to explain himself to a mere constable.

"Well, you can always tell me, old bean, and I'll pass it along," Percy beamed and Clara noted the gleam she had half expected in his expression. Knowing Percy he would already be looking at ways to get into the inspector's good books and a lead on a case would be just right.

"Won't do, Percy," Clara said, making her voice sound forlorn. "Tommy made me promise I would only speak to the Inspector."

A shadow fell over Percy's expression.

"Tommy, huh?" Percy's eyes seemed to be staring everywhere at once, which was fairly easy for a young man with his condition. "I heard he was back but not so fit. Can turn a man's head all that blood and violence. Tommy all right, is he?"

Clara sensed his trepidation.

"He does all right, gets about quite well considering."

"Mobile then, is he?"

"Oh yes and travels all about. Mind you, he sometimes worries me when that temper takes hold of him."

"Temper?" Percy looked uneasy.

"Quite frightful when he gets in one of his moods and takes against someone, and then no one can stop him from going to find them and having it out. He gets this determined look in his eyes. I have had to search all over Brighton for him at times," Clara was quite enjoying her creation of the 'monstrous Tommy' and the effect it was clearly having on Percy.

"Still, don't suppose he can do much damage as he is," Percy said in a tone that suggested he was trying to reassure himself.

"No, well not *alone*, he can't," Clara laid her emphasis heavy. "He always did have a lot of friends though."

"Oh yes, lots of friends Tommy always had," Percy was uneasy. "And he said, er, that you should only speak to the Inspector?"

"Yes, but I suppose he wouldn't be too displeased if I told you. I mean you can pass the message on and you were one of Tommy's pals, weren't you?"

"Definitely," Percy had a glazed look as he was remembering the sight of Tommy Fitzgerald angry with him because he had made Clara cry.

Then he made up his mind.

"Look here, sergeant. I think we should let the Inspector hear the girl out. I'll escort her up and take responsibility if you like."

The sergeant gave a noncommittal shrug, his eyes looking a little too shrewdly at Clara who was doing her best not to smile.

"As you wish," he shrugged.

With that, Percy was leading the way upstairs.

"You'll tell Tommy I helped, won't you?" He asked as they entered a dark corridor with doors leading off it on either side.

"Certainly. I shall sing your praises to him and I am sure he would like to visit an old friend. He knows where your ma's house is, doesn't he?"

"Oh, I don't live there anymore," Percy said quickly as he knocked at an office door and ushered Clara through. "Miss Fitzgerald to see you, Inspector."

Percy almost raced back out the door, shutting it firmly behind him.

"Are you in the habit of intimidating officers of the law, Miss Fitzgerald?" The inspector asked drily as he looked up from his papers.

"Not wittingly," Clara lied.

"You never do anything unwittingly, Miss Fitzgerald," the inspector replied, motioning to a chair in which he expected her to sit. "I am informed you paid a visit to the Greengage residence yesterday. Mind explaining that to me?"

Clara's mind flicked to Oliver, perturbed that he had given her away.

"I was paying my respects."

"Try again. The neighbour says you claimed to be from some Spiritualist Society and asked to talk to Mr Greengage. Miss Fitzgerald, may I remind you that you are not a police detective and you should stay out of men's business?"

Clara bristled, her whole skin pricked at the insult. She had to take a deep breath before she could give a calm answer.

"Now you have offered me your advice, perhaps we could discuss what I came here for."

"I might as well be talking out of my ars..." the inspector caught himself. "My posterior."

"That is your own business. It is perfectly acceptable for a private detective to investigate a case on behalf of their client, which is what I am doing. My gender is of no concern."

"You are the first female private investigator I ever heard of."

"I don't doubt I will have to prove myself to you and many others, Inspector," Clara became serious. "I knew that perfectly well the moment I decided to start my business, but then there is very little in this life that a woman doesn't have to prove herself in. Even as a nurse during the war, the male doctors were all patronising buffoons who thought us girls had just been wrangled in from the nearest dance hall."

The inspector smiled weakly and leaned back in his chair.

"Your point is made," he assured her. "Perhaps you're right and women will make fine detectives. God knows you lot are certainly nosy enough."

Clara didn't rise to the bait, she had more dignity.

"You want to discuss this case then?" The inspector suggested to break the stony silence he was receiving. "By the way, I have officially taken you off my suspects' list."

"Jolly good, and what about Mrs Wilton?"

"That old cat's still on the top of my agenda. Dead fishy it is spending all your time searching for a lost treasure your deceased husband has supposedly told you about through the agency of a clairvoyant."

"I don't deny it is odd, but many people believe in women like Mrs Greengage, especially since the war."

"Mrs Wilton is a funny one, but I take it you are trying to prove her innocent?" The inspector steepled his fingers under his chin.

"More precisely, I am looking for Mrs Greengage's murderer, which may, indeed, prove Mrs Wilton's innocence."

"So you are not sure yourself?"

"I am keeping an open-mind, which I believe is the typical police approach."

"Quite," the inspector paused, "I expected a woman to be more..."

"Emotional?" Clara suggested.

"More inclined to stick up for one of her own."

"We, women I mean, are not a club or secret society, Inspector, and I take my work very seriously."

"I can see that. So what is it you wanted to talk about?"

Clara was relieved to be finally getting back to business.

"You tested Augustus the parrot for poison and he came back full of strychnine. Why did you think to test him, may I ask?"

"Just a hunch really. Dropping down dead like that just before his mistress did the same seemed rather suspicious. In my line of work coincidences are less common than mistakes made to look like them."

"But Mrs Greengage wasn't poisoned."

"No, but our doctor down here had seen a bird die like that before from poison. He recognised the signs, and as I had already told him I was suspicious about the bird's death, he decided to test the corpse for foreign chemicals."

"So that is clear, but now tell me, did you test the sherry?"

There was a flicker of uncertainty on the inspector's face.

"As you say, the woman was shot," he said as he reached for a pile of brown cardboard folders. "Even if we found the poison, it wouldn't convict the murderer, unless you are thinking of sending this matter to the RSPCA."

"You know as well as I do Inspector that how the poison came to be in the parrot could be a vital clue."

"It had to be in the sherry, no other option," the inspector was thumbing through papers now.

"I agree. But the murderer took a terrible risk. He could have killed any of us. It was clumsy at best."

"Or audacious," the inspector suddenly relaxed. "Here it is."

He held a piece of paper towards Clara, smiling in a manner she considered rather self-satisfied. She read the laboratory report he had just handed her.

"There was no poison in the sherry," she put the paper down in amazement. "Can there have been a mistake?"

"It does seem a little curious, but our chemist is highly regarded and reliable. If he says the sherry was clear, it must be."

Clara couldn't believe her eyes; she had been convinced the sherry was the medium for the poison. Or had she been? Why had she pushed so hard to find out if she was so certain, after all? No, that doubt had been there already and now it was confirmed.

"Poison in the parrot but not in the sherry."

"Certainly puzzling, though it explains why the rest of you were fine. I am tracing strychnine sales in the local area of course," the inspector took back his piece of paper a little too gleefully for Clara's liking. "Anything else I can help you with?"

Clara pulled her thoughts back together. This was important she felt, but she could assess the implications when she was back home. Right now she had to concentrate; she might not get another opportunity to grill the inspector.

"There was one other thing. I was told that Mrs Greengage had to move to Brighton from Eastbourne because she had accused someone of murder. Could you get me the details?"

The inspector returned to leaning his chin on his hands.

"I expect I could. I don't think it's connected though. She was just an old busy-body."

"Or someone who knew something but was afraid to reveal how she knew."

"That is typical female thinking, over-complicating everything," the inspector shook his head.

"Then I suppose I am also over-thinking when I consider it peculiar that the riddles have gone missing?"

"Riddles? What riddles?"

Clara enjoyed a moment to feel satisfied that she knew more than the inspector.

"The riddles Mrs Greengage had been communicating to Mrs Wilton via her, ahem, mediumship. There were nine, I believe, but Mrs Wilton only ever received three, and now the other six have vanished."

"Then that only strengthens the case against Mrs Wilton."

"Except she came to me on the very morning of the murder, after you had interviewed her, to ask me to retrieve the remaining riddles for her. Which I tried to, only to discover they were gone," Clara explained calmly. "She would hardly send me after them if she had already stolen them."

"Unless it was to cast suspicion off of her – a double bluff."

"Inspector, I think both you and I can agree that Mrs Wilton is not that clever a woman."

The inspector thought about this a moment and then sighed.

"So now we have theft to add to the list. This just gets better and better."

"It may also throw new light on the motive for Mrs Greengage's murder."

"I should have known having a woman involved in this would make my life harder. You should meet my wife. You would get on well."

"If you don't mind my saying Inspector, she must be a remarkable woman."

The inspector huffed.

"I'll call back in a couple of days for those details," she added, collecting her gloves and hat.

The inspector grumbled something under his breath and got up to open the door for her.

"Oh, one last thing," Clara paused. "A strange man followed me home yesterday. I didn't like the look of him."

"You are letting this detective business go to your head," the inspector replied. "Go home and carry on with your investigating if it pleases you."

Clara was annoyed at the dismissal of her worries and as she walked down the stairs of the station, the inspector's words rolled around her mind. Could he be right and she was making something out of nothing? Perhaps the man behind her *had* been a simple coincidence and she had let her thoughts of murder go to her head. She hoped that was not the case, she considered herself more rational than that. But the inspector was right. Why would anyone follow her?

She exited the police station and anxiously looked up and down the road. There were no mysterious strangers, only an old woman with her shopping in a basket and a young mother pushing an infant in a pram. It seemed the inspector was right about one thing and her follower had been all in her imagination.

Even so she couldn't quite shake her anxiety, and it suddenly seemed a long, lonely walk home, especially when she was looking over her shoulder all the way.

Chapter Thirteen

Annie met her at the door looking worried.

"He's having one of his 'dos'," she said quickly as Clara came in.

"What brought it on this time?" Clara asked, discarding her coat and hat.

"Don't rightly know," Annie was a bundle of nerves. "He insisted on going out, you know how he hates being stuck indoors. I only left him a moment by the bandstand while I bought two teas."

"It isn't your fault Annie," Clara rubbed the girl's arm. "It is one of those things the war has left us ladies to deal with. I think the War Office assumes that is all we are here for, to pick up the pieces. He will be all right."

Annie headed back to the kitchen looking upset, while Clara headed for the parlour.

Tommy was sat at the table, head in hands. A newspaper and a magazine had been ripped to pieces and lay scattered about the floor. Something had been flung at the wall cracking a picture frame, though Clara counted her lucky stars it had missed the huge fireplace mirror just next to it. As she entered the room, her feet crunched on something, and she looked down at the remains of a tea cup and saucer.

"Go away, Annie," Tommy said gruffly, not looking up.

"It isn't Annie," Clara stalked across the room. "Have you been redecorating?"

"Go away."

"Not if you are going to throw tea cups around again."

Clara sank into the nearest armchair and waited. Several moments passed.

"Are you just going to sit there?" Tommy snapped.

"It seems likely."

By now Clara was used to her brother's outbursts triggered by anything as random as a dead cat by the road or the smell of frying bacon. She also knew that taking a sympathetic approach only deepened Tommy's self-pity and loathing. Instead she had to snap him out of it as speedily as possible by standing for no nonsense. The nurses at the hospital had termed the process 'jollying' a person up.

Tommy suddenly snatched up a teaspoon and twisted back his arm to throw it.

"Don't you dare!" Clara told him in a tone that sounded all too much like her mother for comfort.

"You don't know how it feels!" Tommy yelled.

"No, but I know how hard it is to get dents out of a teaspoon, and I am fed up rummaging in Mr Morton's junk shop for old tea cups just so I can afford for you to break them. So kindly put down that spoon."

Tommy hesitated. There was a long pause where the teaspoon's fate hung perilously in the balance. Then, with exquisite care, he put it down.

"You've been buying old tea cups at Morton's? How many have I broken?" He asked stiffly.

"Sixteen."

The danger was passing, and Clara began to relax.

"It just gets to me some days," Tommy sank his head into his hands. "And then I just want to yell and shout and break things. I feel as if I keep it all bottled up any longer, I'll just go insane."

"I know," Clara spoke softly. "So what sparked it this time?"

"Eric Sprigg," Tommy shrugged. "He didn't mean to."

"Clerk at the biscuit factory, isn't he?"

"Yes. And he spotted me at the park. He just wanted to talk about old times. He wasn't to know. He has hopes to start the county cricket team up again."

Clara understood. Before the war, Tommy had been a champion cricketer. It had even been said he could play for a national team. There had been debate whether Tommy would continue his academic studies or try his hand at playing for England. But the war had ended that debate.

"He was so eager to pick my brains," Tommy snorted. "And tell me all about his problems finding enough able-bodied men willing to play. If Annie hadn't returned at that point, I think I might have socked him one right in his smiling face."

Tommy fingered his useless legs, legs that had once carried him across the green grass of a cricket pitch and now could barely carry him from his bed to his wheelchair.

"It was ill-manners on Eric's part. I don't suppose he thought how it would affect you."

"No one does," Tommy wrapped his head back in his hands. "Some days it's like the war never happened and everyone is trying too hard to behave as if everything is normal, but it's not normal. I will never be normal again."

"On that I don't agree with you," Clara walked to him and gently stroked his hair. "Now come on, we've worried Annie long enough."

"Poor Annie," Tommy woke momentarily from his slump, then he sank again. "I wonder she puts up with an old crock like me."

"It must be love," Clara said lightly enough, but Tommy's head shot up.

"What do you mean?"

"Well, she hardly puts up with you for the pittance I can afford to pay her."

That did the trick. Tommy was too distracted to continue moping about his own woes. Clara decided to maintain the diversions.

"So, are you ready to hear my news?"

Tommy glanced at her.

"What news?"

"There was no strychnine in the sherry. Augustus was not poisoned that way."

"Actually, I am quite relieved. It has been on my mind that we all came very close to a nasty end, but now we know it wasn't just good fortune that kept us alive."

"Yes, but it leaves us no closer to an answer," Clara sighed. "I was thinking..."

A knock on the door interrupted her. A head appeared.

"I thought it sounded calmer," Annie edged nervously around the door. "Are you better Tommy?"

"Course Annie," Tommy pulled out a big smile for her. "You must take no notice of me when I have these silly moods."

Annie merely nodded.

"I'll get dinner on then."

She vanished.

"She's still upset," Tommy sighed.

"She will get over that too," Clara assured him.

Tommy drifted into thought again, then roused himself visibly.

"You were saying?"

"I am thinking I need to spread my net wider, as the saying goes, and see what suspects I can catch. I've asked the Inspector to get information for me on that old case Mrs Greengage was involved in, but I wouldn't mind a trip to her old neighbourhood in Eastbourne to make some enquires."

"You think that will help?"

"I don't know, but in my experience a good neighbour, and by that I mean one who is dreadfully nosy, often knows far more about a person than any policeman can discover. Besides, I don't trust the Inspector to tell me everything."

Tommy looked at her curiously, and she felt expected to explain.

"He thinks I am just a woman who is too bored to do anything else but sniff around in his business."

"Then he's a fool."

"Yes, but he is the fool who is in authority. Trust me, Tommy, when I say I know what it is like to feel useless and left out."

Tommy looked mildly abashed.

"Hope I never caused you to feel that way, old thing."

"Oh Tommy, of course you have, but you couldn't help it. You're just a man, and society teaches you how to treat women."

"Well, this last year or so has taught me that a lot of things in this life are not as they ought to be. I have faith that you can solve this case, and anything I can do to help I shall."

Clara considered for a moment.

"Are you up for a train ride?"

"Always. I haven't been on a train since they shipped me home, and that wasn't exactly a joyful ride."

"Then I'll inform Annie, and tomorrow we will be up early and heading for Eastbourne."

Chapter
Fourteen

I t took Clara a late evening visit to Mrs Wilton, and lots of words of comfort that she was not about to face the hangman, to discover Mrs Greengage's old address in Eastbourne. It was fortunate that Mrs Wilton had such a nose for details and gossip. At least it saved having to disturb the grieving widower, though Clara was contemplating another conversation with him anyway as soon as she could.

The trains were back running on their old timetables since the war, so there was little difficulty getting tickets for Eastbourne. Though getting Tommy in his cumbersome wheelchair on the train was another matter. The step into the carriage and the narrow doorway made it seem an impossible task before the train pulled out of the station. Only the assistance of a railway porter saved the day. Clearly it was not the first wheelchair he had loaded, because as soon as Tommy was aboard he found some heavy wooden blocks to put in front of the wheels of the chair to prevent it rolling forward.

Clara breathed a sigh of relief as she settled into a horse-hair padded seat. Annie perched opposite her.

"I made egg sandwiches," she said as a whistle rang out and the train heaved into motion. "For when we get peckish."

Annie was still a tad unclear on the purpose for their trip and imagined it was something to pull Tommy out of his mood. She had organised a luncheon like they were going on a picnic and was wearing her best hat. Clara thought it was perhaps time to properly explain their objective.

"Annie, you know all this business about Mrs Greengage?"

"That's all anyone talks about," Annie nodded.

"Well, I am doing a little bit of my own detective work into the case, for the sake of..." how to refer to Mrs Wilton discreetly? "...a friend."

"What she means Annie is that we are going to a place called Oakham Avenue in Eastbourne to be terribly nosy and ask lots of questions about the deceased," Tommy butted in.

"This is not about being nosy. This is proper detective work and very important. So you mustn't tell a soul Annie."

Annie was looking a little bewildered.

"If it makes you feel better, Annie, the police know all about what I am doing," Clara bent the truth only slightly.

"So what is important about Oakham Avenue?" The maid asked.

"Mrs Greengage used to live there," Tommy elaborated. "And Clara is after some background information."

"Background?" Clara glanced at him.

"Yes, the stuff in a person's past. It was a term used in that detective book."

"So things like Mr Greengage being in the music halls before the war?" Annie said.

They both looked at her.

"Where did you hear that?"

"Dr Macpherson's tweenie maid. She does occasional outside work, including weekly cleaning at the Greengages' house. She was dusting the writing desk once, and it fell open, accidentally."

"Of course," Tommy nodded insincerely.

"Well, inside were all these old posters from music halls, and Mr Greengage was on them. Though looking all dressed up for the stage, of course. The posters claimed he was very good. Used to sing and do the ven-tilly-thing, where someone throws their voice."

A cog slipped into place in Clara's mind. The strange powers Augustus displayed now made sense. But it opened another thought as well. If a maid could walk in and find theatre posters in the writing desk, then she could also find those riddles.

"What is this maid's name?"

"Alice," Annie shrugged. "That's all I know her by."

It wasn't much, but if Clara could discover whether Alice had been at the house on the day of the murder, it might just explain the loss of the riddles.

"An interesting thought just come to you, old thing?" Tommy queried when he noticed the distant look on Clara's face.

"More than one actually," Clara replied. "But there are still so many gaps. Oh well, let's keep at it."

The train rumbled on, the scenery flicking by and changing from town to countryside and then back to town. They arrived at Eastbourne and asked directions to Oakham Avenue. Thankfully, it wasn't a long walk, and the women took turns pushing Tommy to share the load.

"So where do we begin?" Annie looked up at the red brick terrace houses of Oakham Avenue. They were grander than Mrs Greengage's current property, and the obvious conclusion was that the clairvoyant had gone down in the world. Was that because she was running from someone or because her financial circumstances had changed? Now

Clara knew more about Mr Greengage, she was inclined to believe the latter.

"You start at that end of the road, I'll start this end and we can meet in the middle," Clara directed.

"Righty-ho," Tommy grinned cheerfully. "First to find a suspect can treat us all to a sticky bun."

"Do take this seriously," Clara heard Annie whisper to him as they headed down the street.

Clara started at number 49 which looked a little on the worn side and proved to be owned by a retired major who had only been in the area a month. Number 47 also proved to have recent new tenants as it was a rented property. Number 45 was empty, and so the story continued as she worked her way down the row. Finally, at number 39, she was greeted by a maid who responded to her initial queries with confirmation that her mistress had been living there many years, though was not sure the exact number.

She ushered Clara into a front parlour and went to see if her mistress was free to talk. It was slightly improper. The maid should have checked first before asking her in, but first appearances at the house suggested it was a place where informality was welcomed.

The front room was littered with the remnants of the occupant's activities. A flower press stood open on a table beside a scrapbook. A half-finished embroidery was flung on a chair by the fireplace, the needle loose and hanging precariously from a thread over the edge. Clara desperately wanted to snatch it up and secure it in the fabric before it was lost.

A sketchy watercolour of more flowers stood forlornly in the window, surrounded by other incomplete drawings. In fact Clara suspected this was a house where nothing was ever finished properly. Books stood in stacks by the table, some open or containing torn paper for page markers. Clara picked one up and read the title – *Spiritualism in the Modern Age*. It seemed she had stumbled on just the right household.

Abruptly the door flung open, and a woman appeared in what could be best described as Arabian costume. She wore strange loose trousers and a drapery of shawls about her shoulders and head. Beads dripped off her in coral reds and deep blues. She entered the room with a flourish that allowed Clara to see she was bare-footed. It was all very theatrical and, in Clara's mind, quite silly.

"Clara Fitzgerald," she offered her hand as the maid had not reappeared to introduce her.

"Madame Delmont," the woman stood before her, pressed her hands together like she was praying, and took a deep bow.

Clara was now beginning to think this was not the right house at all.

"My maid says you are making enquiries about a former resident in our road?" Madame Delmont said airily. "Do be seated."

Clara aimed for the chair by the fireplace and took the opportunity to remove the piece of offending sewing, while Madame Delmont descended onto a sofa bed near the window.

"I am making enquiries on behalf of an interested party about a lady named Mrs Greengage," Clara began.

"Her!" Delmont sat up suddenly. "Real old bag of wind she was. What has she done?"

Clara took a moment before deciding not to reveal the murder – such revelations had a tendency to stilt conversation.

"It was a problem over a reading, I believe," Clara replied vaguely. "And Mrs Greengage is no longer available to rectify the problem."

"That doesn't surprise me, she is a sly one and as I always told her, it does not do to charge for the talents one has been freely given."

"You mean her psychic abilities?"

"Yes. Though if you ask me there was a little something 'forced' about them. I know these things, I am an adept myself you see."

"An adept?" Clara tried to mask her scepticism.

"Oh yes, in spiritual matters. I have travelled all over the East to learn my skills. It quite grated on my nerves to see that home-grown witch plying her talent as though it was a parlour game. You have to take these things seriously or else the Spirits will come for you."

That was uncomfortably close to home.

"So you didn't like her?"

"Didn't like is rather harsh. I was concerned for her, and I didn't approve of what she was doing."

"I see."

"I take it she has passed on false information?" Madame Delmont was looking rather keen now, clearly having a spiritual talent did not prevent you from being a gossip.

"Well, that is the thing, the lady I am making enquiries for isn't sure what to make of the information, and it seems some of it may have been withheld."

"I knew it!" Delmont slapped her thighs with excitement. "I always said she was using her skills to drag people along and make money. It was all so much show you see. Everything from her clothes to the room she gave readings in."

Clara glanced at Madame Delmont's clothes, but said nothing.

"I blame the husband of course. He was on the stage. She was always using some sort of novelty to lure in trade."

"Like Augustus the parrot?" Clara offered.

Madame Delmont looked blank.

"I don't recall a parrot, but I remember for a time she had a crystal ball, of all things! Then there was the witch's ball hung at the door and the shawl embroidered with occult symbols that she liked to claim was a gift from a Red Indian Chieftain. Of course there are those that are impressed by all that, and *they* flocked to her."

Chapter Fifteen

M adame Delmont wrinkled her nose as though she had smelt something bad. But the picture she was painting of Mrs Greengage was certainly interesting.

"Did you ever hear about her producing riddles from the dead?"

"No," Delmont shrugged. "Though it sounds the sort of thing she would do."

"And were there any scandals resulting from her use of novelties?" Clara persisted.

"Not that I remember," Madame Delmont tapped her lips with one finger. "It was very irritating how she always managed to get away with her charades."

Clara recognised jealousy when it was before her, but it didn't seem to add up to Delmont being a suspect, and it certainly didn't tell her about the crime Mrs Greengage supposedly uncovered.

"I was under the impression," she said carefully, "that it was some sort of scandal that made Mrs Greengage leave Eastbourne and go to Brighton."

"No, that wasn't one of her novelties," Delmont paused. "That was far more serious. It was the one thing I agreed with her on."

"I don't quite understand."

"She came to me one evening, it must have been the November before last and she was in an awful state. For a second or two, I quite thought she had lost her mind. She was talking some strange story about receiving a message from the Spirits quite out of the blue and was dreadfully disturbed by it. I let her talk, what else could I do? She sat exactly where you are and said 'I just had a vision of a murder'."

"Really?" Clara was trying to picture the scene and found it all so preposterous.

"She was very sincere. I made her a cup of tea and asked her to explain. She said she had been pulling a joint of mutton out of the oven when this terrible pain hit her between the eyes and then she saw this woman being poisoned. She saw the culprit clear as day. I was quite astonished because I had always thought her powers a bit..."

"Forced?" Clara reminded her.

"Did I say that? Well, yes that was it. After all, if anyone was to witness a murder, spiritually speaking, it should really have been me. I have, after all, been trained in the art of dream-walking and advanced mesmerisation by a Chinese monk."

"And these things are important?"

"It means I can memorise a dream and replay it any time in my head. You can see how that would be useful in a murder case."

If you had the dream, Clara thought to herself, only you didn't and Mrs Greengage, the charlatan, did.

"Then what?" Clara asked.

"She drank her tea and went home. I had convinced her you see that it was all a hallucination brought on by over-work," Delmont smiled a little. "I mean, I could hardly credit that she had had a genuine vision. But then she was back the next day with the newspaper, waving it under my nose and making such a scene. She said it was there in black and white – woman found dead in mysterious circumstances – and what was more she had had another vision that gave her the name of the man who had killed her."

Clara sat up straight, fascinated despite her scepticism.

"The murderer was not named in the papers?"

"I thought about that myself, but no, no suspect was named. I really didn't know what to say, and she was desperate to know if I thought she should go to the police," Madame Delmont looked suddenly shy and fiddled with an edge of the strange eastern costume. "I confess I wasn't in the best mood that day and I was feeling rather..."

Madame Delmont let out a faint groan of regret.

"I was jealous," she said. "And I told her to go to the police because I knew they wouldn't take her seriously and she would be laughed at."

"And did she go?" Clara asked neutrally.

"Yes, and blow me, if they didn't take her seriously, but what could they do without evidence? When they announced they could make no arrests, she was livid and started telling everyone she met the name of the murderer."

"I imagine he was pleased."

"I can't say, I never met him," Delmont reclined back in her chair. "Actually now you mention it a man did call on her, but I don't recall the whole matter, just a lot of shouting. Of course, the scandal ruined her reputation, and no one would visit her anymore. I think it was her lack of discretion that upset people. I mean, going around naming a man a murderer is just awful, isn't it?"

"I was under the impression she was afraid of the man she named?" Clara hinted.

"If she was it certainly didn't stop her speaking about him everywhere she went. I do know her husband was quite appalled and he found the move very difficult."

"He has close ties to Eastbourne?"

"No, but he came back from the war in a bad way and just refused to leave the house ever again. Effectively prevented him working, so I suppose that is why Mrs Greengage took up the séances. She didn't do them before the war."

"But eventually he had to leave the house."

"Certainly, but only with a good dose of morphine inside him I dare say. Only saw him briefly as he was helped into the moving men's cart. He hid himself up in the back. A lot of that sort of behaviour is in the mind, you know."

Clara made no comment.

"The more I think about it, the more I am convinced they were a really odd pair," Madame Delmont flicked the red and blue beads.

"Well, thank you for taking the time to talk to me," Clara stood from her seat.

"Sorry I couldn't be more help," Madame Delmont didn't move. "Let yourself out, won't you?"

Clara tutted under her breath and fudged on her gloves. As she reached the door, she paused.

"I don't suppose you remember the name of the man Mrs Greengage accused of murder?"

"Wait a moment," Madame Delmont tapped her chin. "Yes, actually, I think it was Mr Hansom, like the cabs."

"Thank you," Clara said, letting herself out.

On the pavement she continued to fidget with her gloves, her mind racing over all the information she had just been told. This Mr Hansom had to be a suspect, a far better one than Mrs Wilton.

She was glancing up the street looking for Tommy, when she saw *him*. It was only for a second. He was standing at the end of an alley between two houses and looking straight across at Clara. In that instant, she was certain it was the man who had followed her the other night. Then Tommy called her name, and she turned instinctively. By the time, she looked back the man was gone.

"Any luck?" Tommy called.

"A little," Clara said, unable to take her eyes off the empty alley.

"Been a bit of a dead end for us, I'm afraid," Tommy replied. "Several houses had no one home but the servants, and most of the others never had much to do with Mrs Greengage so couldn't help. Mrs Rimpton at number 23 had called on her neighbour when she wanted to get in contact with her late cat, but apparently Mrs Greengage wasn't agreeable on the matter."

"So she had some limits? I propose we head back for the train if everyone is happy and I will tell you what I learned," Clara prised her eyes from the alley, telling herself it was a trick of the light or her memory.

"I saw they serve teas at the station," Annie said helpfully.

"I quite fancied that Lyons teashop we passed on the way here," countered Tommy.

"Have you seen their prices since the war?" Annie cocked her head on one side and looked scolding.

"A man doesn't get luxuries like that very often."

"Luxuries? I call it a luxury if I can get soap enough to do the weekly wash!"

Clara only half-listened to them playfully arguing. Her mind was on the strange figure. It was preposterous that she might be followed and even more so that her stalker would trail her here. After all, he would have had to get on her train, which meant he had been watching her house to see where she would go. Otherwise, he could not have known she was going to Eastbourne. Clara worried at the idea. It was ridiculous, but it was even more so to believe that a complete stranger could turn up in the same place as herself twice in a row. So perhaps she was seeing things?

Except... except he had just vanished as if he didn't want to be noticed and he had been looking directly at her, of that she was certain.

Clara shuddered. Maybe she should tell Tommy, but the inspector had thought she was being silly and maybe her brother would too? She sighed. Perhaps after all she was just becoming paranoid.

Hurrying, she caught up with Annie and Tommy and discovered her brother had won the argument and they were heading for the Lyons teashop. As they walked on, Clara only had the courage to look over her shoulder once.

Chapter Sixteen

I t was rather early to be knocking on a person's door, but Clara had a lot to do today and felt bold enough to risk being impolite. Mr Greengage opened the door, looking a little worried.

"I do apologise for the earliness of this visit Mr Greengage. You remember me from the Spiritualist Society?"

Mr Greengage hesitated for a moment and fiddled with the buttons on his waistcoat where a fresh yellow egg stain lingered. He touched the damp spot and absent-mindedly put his finger to his mouth to lick off the mess.

"I came just after your wife's sad departure," Clara clarified.

Mr Greengage's face sank.

"Oh, yes."

"I wanted to check you were doing all right. I have an appointment in the area later, and as I was passing, I thought I would drop by."

"That's very kind," Mr Greengage pulled at his buttons again. "Would you care to come in?"

Clara nodded her assent and, to her horror, Mr Greengage led her through into the front parlour where only two days before his wife's cold body had lain. Clara froze on the threshold, her eyes unerringly seeking out the blood stain on the rug and finding it. The man hadn't bothered to even move the rug! Clara felt her stomach turn.

On the table, where Mrs Greengage had given her last séance, sat a half-eaten plate of bacon and eggs. Clara was so stunned that for a moment, she forgot that she wasn't supposed to know the murder had occurred in this very room.

"You eat in here?" Her voice sounded sharp to her ears.

"It gets the best light in the mornings."

Clara regained her composure, reminding herself that Mr Greengage was just a rather peculiar man and that she was supposed to be a sympathetic friend of his late wife.

"I was brought up that front rooms were only for births, marriages and funerals," she had meant the comment to explain her consternation, but as soon as the words slipped out, she couldn't believe how tactless they sounded.

Fortunately Mr Greengage seemed oblivious.

"My mother was like that. What nonsense! Why have a room and not use it, I say. Do take a seat."

For a moment Clara thought her feet wouldn't move, then she shoved her emotions firmly down in the pit of her belly and, with great effort, sat down in a chair. She resolutely avoided looking at the blood stain.

"I see you are doing as well as can be expected," Clara spoke, aware her throat felt tight around each word.

"It's lonely, but I get by," Mr Greengage replied. "People have been very kind, but I really don't know what I shall do now. I suppose you are aware that my dear Martha paid all our bills with her talents?"

"I was aware you had had… complications."

"Doctors call it Agoraphobia. It's a nervous disorder that means I can't stand being in big open spaces. Just stepping outside the house has me trembling with fear. When the police made me leave while they were investigating, I thought I would die," he shuddered. "I was so relieved to get back inside these four walls."

"It doesn't bother you that your wife... died... here?"

"I don't really think about it. Mostly I just sit and worry about what the future holds," Mr Greengage gazed forlornly at his plate.

Clara felt a wave of pity for this poor, strange man. He looked so miserable, so lost, yet she could offer no solution to him.

"How long is it since you last worked?"

"Before the war," Mr Greengage jabbed his fork into the remains of egg white. "I was on the stage, you know? I was quite well-known in my time. Performed in a lot of end-of-the-pier shows. There was even talk of going to London, but then the war came. Everything changed after that. I was injured and lay in No Man's Land for two days. When they found me, apparently I was completely out of my mind. I was screaming and raving. All I remember is the shrieking of the shells going over and the popping of the guns. I lay in constant fear of a shell landing near me, and all I could see was this big open sky, knowing that at any moment a shell could fall out of it and finish me. When I recovered, I could no longer face open spaces."

Clara was listening to his story, but her thoughts had slipped to Tommy. He had never really spoken about his war experiences. She pictured him lying alone in No Man's Land, and her stomach clenched painfully.

"I'm sorry. I have made you sad."

Clara looked up in surprise at the comment from Mr Greengage. She abruptly realised there were tears running down her face.

"I am fine," she fumbled for a handkerchief. "I was just thinking of my brother. He had a similar ordeal to you in the war."

"Is he all right?"

"Not entirely, no," Clara put away the handkerchief, ferociously determined to shed no further tears.

"Let me show you something from a better time," Mr Greengage tapped her hand and escorted her into the study. Clara was only too pleased to get out of the parlour.

Mr Greengage went to the big writing desk and pulled down the front. From it he drew a pile of posters and handed them to Clara. She looked at the first one. It was black with boxy red letters and a face drawn in semi-silhouette. She recognised the features as an earlier version of Mr Greengage.

"That was my first headline performance," he explained.

She flicked to the next poster; this one was rather plainer. On a beige background, a black and white figure in a dinner suit lifted his arms to an audience of dogs, cats, and birds. In orange and black letters, the poster declared: "The Miraculous Dr Greengage! Makes Animals Talk!"

Clara glanced at her host curiously.

"My gimmick was giving voices to animals," Mr Greengage smiled sheepishly. "I could do all different voices. It was quite a gift. The cats spoke slowly and smoothly with a hint of disdain. The dogs always sounded jolly and keen, and the birds always spoke fast and in short sentences. I drew quite a crowd. Some people actually believed I had taught the animals to talk."

Clara turned to the last poster. It was much older, and Mr Greengage was not yet declared an honorary doctor. In fact he was only a side act and introduced as Greengage the Ventriloquist. Clara nodded thoughtfully at the posters and then handed them all back.

"Happier times," she remarked.

"They certainly were that."

"I can't help but noticing, excuse the impertinence, but you had birds in your act and your wife also had access to, from what I have heard, a very unique parrot."

Mr Greengage carefully returned the posters to the desk and clicked it shut.

"Augustus was indeed different."

"As I said, unique. Perhaps you trained him?" Clara pushed.

"You are not a stupid woman, I can see that, and I suppose trying to persuade you that Augustus was a fortunate freak of nature would be unlikely to succeed?"

Clara smiled gently.

"I understand times are hard, Mr Greengage. Businesses all need their little novelties and devices to draw customers in. I am not here to judge your motives or condemn you."

"It was so logical, or so it seemed. The move from Eastbourne lost Martha all her clients, and she had to start afresh. She needed something to make her standout from the competition," Mr Greengage shook his head wistfully. "Augustus was a relic from the old days. Pre-war. He had seen some places, that bird. He could ride a tiny bicycle. I bought him off a retired animal trainer. I gave him his voice."

Mr Greengage went quiet.

"I guessed as much," Clara nodded, it wasn't much of a clue but it felt as though another piece of the puzzle had slipped into place. "There was one other thing I needed to mention to you."

The worry returned to Mr Greengage's face.

"The riddles I took from you the other day to give to Mrs Wilton? They were all blank. Perhaps you gave me the wrong envelope?"

"No, no! They were the correct papers. I remembered seeing them only the night before..." Mr Greengage seemed genuinely surprised. "How can they be missing?"

"It appears someone took the real riddles and replaced them with blank slips of paper. Do you have a maid?" Clara knew the answer, but she wanted to hear it from him.

"No. Well. Yes. A girl comes in occasionally to clean. You think...?"

"All I am suggesting is that she may have moved them accidentally."

"Alice Roberts," Mr Greengage said firmly. "In fact she came in the very morning... She always cleaned the front parlour last. She knew where the spare key was kept and would let herself in. It was convenient with my wife sometimes working late, and those damn sleeping draughts knocking me out cold for hours. She was the one who found the body."

"And then she woke you?"

"Actually, that's the thing. She rushed clean out of the house and fetched another girl. It was this stranger who woke me. I did tell the police this, but the girl had an alibi."

"For the murder at least," Clara muttered to herself, then, louder, "How long was it between her finding the body and running for her friend, then waking you, do you suppose?"

"How should I know?" Mr Greengage laughed grimly. "She's a cool character that one, never even screamed when she found the body. I suppose she took the riddles before waking me?"

"Perhaps," Clara refused to commit herself further. "Thank you for your time Mr Greengage."

"It has been my pleasure," Greengage smiled. "I presume you know the funeral is tomorrow? Afraid it's not the Spiritualists but old Reverend Gregg at St. Peters who is conducting it."

"Oh, yes," Clara lied.

"I don't expect a large crowd. I won't be there. Too much in the open air," Mr Greengage shivered violently. Clara wasn't certain if it was because of his grief for his wife or the sudden thought of venturing outdoors.

"I'm sure it will be a fine service," Clara patted his hand and then made her excuses so she could be on her way.

She had intended visiting Inspector Park-Coombs as her next stop, but now she was itching to find Alice Roberts. She doubted she would be able to sit still and listen to the inspector when there was a new witness to track down. She compromised by making her way to the nearest teashop and ordering a pot for one. She would sit and drink her tea while her mind settled and she considered her next move.

Was Alice a suspect or merely an opportunistic thief? And who was the friend she had run for? Perhaps Annie would know more. In fact the more she thought about it, the more it occurred to her that this might be a job best suited to Annie altogether. Annie, as a fellow servant, might be able to encourage Alice to talk, whereas Clara's presence would be liable to make her hold her tongue. Servants didn't usually gossip to their employers, but they did talk among themselves.

Clara was just debating whether to pop home and ask Annie to visit Alice at once when a friendly voice called to her. She looked up and was surprised to see Oliver Bankes.

"Oh, hello," she said absently.

"Didn't mean to disturb you."

"I was just lost in thought, that's all. It is a bad habit."

"I just came for a spot of late breakfast. I've been around the corner taking photographs."

"Another murder?" Clara said bleakly.

Oliver laughed.

"No, just wanted to take a shot of the sun rising over the houses. Urban landscape shots are a hobby of mine."

Clara now noticed the heavy tripod and large trunk, like an over-sized suitcase, that Oliver had put down at his feet. A couple of new customers upon entering the teashop, had trouble negotiating past the boxes in the cramped seating area.

"I best find a chair," Oliver looked around the room purposefully.

There wasn't another free seat to be had. Clara realised what was coming and decided her manners would have to take precedence over her meditations.

"Sit here, won't you?"

Oliver's face lit up gratefully.

"Thank you, I always forget how busy this place is," he wedged his belongings between the table and the ornate teashop window, then whistled for a waitress.

"What are you doing here anyway?" He asked after ordering tea and crumpets. He offered to order more tea for Clara but she declined.

"Just carrying on with my investigations," she shrugged casually.

"Any luck?"

"Yes and no."

"You are quite welcome to look over the crime scene photographs at any time."

"Thank you," Clara smiled. "But I don't think that necessary. They can't tell me anymore than I already know."

Oliver was clearly disappointed.

"Well, if you change your mind," his tea and crumpets arrived.

Clara looked at the buttery crumpets that dripped grease as Oliver raised them to his mouth and felt a pang of hunger. She had barely eaten that morning and wandering about in the cold had awoken her appetite. To escape from looking covetously at Oliver's food she glanced out the window, which was when she saw *him* again.

Tall, in a long over-coat with brown hair and a hat, he wasn't much to look at, but it was him alright. She shut her eyes and wished her strange pursuer gone, but when she looked again he was still there. There was no uncertainty left in Clara's mind that she was being followed. This final encounter was too much of a coincidence.

She tried to remain calm, to rationalise the situation, perhaps he lived in this road? But that didn't explain Eastbourne or why he always seemed to be watching her.

"Are you all right?" Oliver asked suddenly. "You have gone rather pale."

"Tell me you see a man standing there, Oliver," Clara spoke without taking her eyes off the man.

"Where?" Oliver looked outside. It was hard to miss who she meant; there was only one man outside.

"He has been following me."

"Do you know him?"

"No, but I am sure he is following me. Inspector Park-Coombs thinks I am imagining it."

But there was no imagining the cold chill that had crept down her spine or the painful spasm of panic deep in her belly.

"Why would he follow you?" Oliver asked logically enough.

"I don't know. I think it might be to do with the murder of Mrs Greengage."

Could her stalker be the murderer? The thought scared her. If he was, was he following her to make sure she didn't discover the truth? Did that mean she was in danger?

Abruptly Oliver was getting to his feet.

"What are you doing?" hissed Clara.

"I'm going to talk to this fellow."

"But you can't!"

"Why not?"

Clara wanted to say because he might have a gun or be violent, or because he might be a murderer, but that wasn't the sort of thing you blurted out in respectable teashops. Besides, she could see that nothing would deter Oliver.

She need not have worried. As soon as Oliver was out the door, the strange man took to his heels and ran off. Oliver set out after him but came back shortly, empty-handed.

"He was definitely watching us," he said breathlessly. "He wouldn't have run like that if he wasn't up to something suspicious."

"Could you escort me to the police station?" Clara asked, hiding her trembling hands in her lap.

"Of course! You are reporting him?"

"For what good it will do," Clara was resigned to the inspector's scorn, but she gladly took Oliver's arm as they left the tearooms.

Chapter Seventeen

Inspector Park-Coombs was on his tea break when Clara arrived and would have refused to see her had Oliver not used his connections with the police to insist she went straight to his office.

"Miss Fitzgerald," he said, putting down a biscuit he had been looking forward to dunking in his tea.

"Inspector," Clara said politely.

"Look here," Oliver butted in. "She is being followed by this very unsavoury character, and I am concerned that your men don't seem to be taking the situation very seriously."

Clara felt herself reddening. She had not planned to have Oliver accompany her to the inspector's office, nor did she like anyone thinking that she needed someone else (a man in particular) to speak up for her. She rather felt that his presence diminished all the effort she had put into convincing the inspector that she was an independent and fully capable person, despite being a woman.

"Mr Bankes," the inspector said coolly, "I was aware of the suspicion Miss Fitzgerald had."

He gave her a look that suggested she was still making a fuss over nothing.

"I take it the matter has become more serious?"

"I saw the dirty fellow!" Oliver stated, jabbing a finger into his chest in emphasis "He looked a real rogue and ran off as soon as I tried to approach him."

"Could be a coincidence," the inspector said drily.

"He turned up at Eastbourne when I was there," Clara responded. "That was a bit far-fetched to be a coincidence."

"He could be the murderer!"

"Calm down, Bankes," the Inspector commanded the young man. "Why don't you go wait downstairs while I have a chat with Miss Fitzgerald?"

"Oh," Oliver glanced at Clara hopeful that she would interject for him to stay, but she declined to say anything. "All right. Shall I wait around to walk you home Clara?"

"No need, Bankes, I'll have one of my boys walk Miss Fitzgerald home. You must be very busy," the inspector laid heavy emphasis on his last sentence, and Oliver mumbled uncomfortably about appointments he had forgotten until that moment and then left abruptly.

"I thought you would prefer a private interview," the inspector said after he was gone.

"He is very sweet," Clara said, finally accepting the chair the inspector offered, "but I really don't need him to fight my corner."

"That I am certain of. But why was he with you?"

"It was just as he said, we saw that man again and I was a little shaken so I asked him to walk me here. I have no idea who this man following me is, Inspector."

"When you first told me about him I was inclined to think you had an over-active imagination."

"Thank you, Inspector," Clara said caustically.

"Let me finish. But my boys have seen him hanging around the crime scene. Same description, youngish, pale over-coat, dark hair, very ordinary looking, but runs off as soon as anyone tries to talk to him."

"So you have no idea who he is either?"

"No. Somehow though, I doubt he is the killer. Most murderers have the sense not to loiter so obviously near the place they committed the crime."

"That doesn't really help much," Clara shook her head.

"I'll have a man escort you home as I promised," Park-Coombs answered. "And I suggest you always go out with company. Never alone. We will catch this fellow sooner or later the way he keeps hanging about. He's probably just a vagrant."

Clara didn't feel particularly comforted but accepted the advice.

"Was there anything else?" Park-Coombs was eyeing up his tea and biscuit.

"You said you would find out about that other case Mrs Greengage was involved with?"

"Oh yes," the inspector shoved his tea to one side forlornly. "I looked into it, as you asked."

"And?"

The inspector settled himself back in his chair and folded his hands over his belly.

"It all began with Mr and Mrs Bundle."

"Ah, Bundle not Bumble!"

"Pardon me?"

"I apologise, Inspector, do carry on."

The inspector sighed heavily.

"The Bundles were a typical Eastbourne couple. She had run a boarding house with her mother while Ted Bundle was a tradesman in the grocery business. When the old mother died Lily Bundle sold the property, which was her inheritance, and suddenly became quite a wealthy woman in her own way.

"She married Ted and lived with him over his shop. From all accounts it was a contented match. They were both in their thirties when they married, but still managed to raise a brood of four children; three girls and a boy.

"The war made things difficult for them and for the first time there were monetary concerns. All the children remained at home, the youngest only just making it into active war service in the last year of the conflict. It was that same year it all went wrong for the Bundles.

"The neighbourhood gossip had it that Ted Bundle made some bad deals and was seriously in debt, close even, to losing the shop. Mrs Bundle could be his saviour with her hidden fortune but it seems Lily was disinclined to help out her husband or at least that was what everyone was saying.

"Then, in November 1918, one of the Bundle girls came home and found her mother stone cold dead in an armchair. Ted was out of town and the post-mortem indicated it was a heart attack, though the coroner couldn't be sure. Lily had always been prone to palpitations anyway.

"No one was particularly surprised or concerned. Lily had looked off-colour lately and the stress of seeing her only son go off to war had apparently been quite telling on her. The funeral was a closed affair with only immediate family and a few neighbours attending. Afterwards everything fell back into its normal flow. Ted ran his shop and was able to pay off his debts with his late wife's estate, but no one thought that odd.

"Then Mrs Greengage came on the scene. Mark my words she was a determined lady. She went to the police claiming she had seen Mr Bundle buying poison at three different chemists. Of course, that was a lie, she had actually 'learned' all this during a séance with the late Mrs Bundle. But she was smart enough to know the police would not take her seriously if she didn't make out that her evidence was first-hand.

"And the police *did* take it seriously. They went after Ted Bundle like hounds after a hare. They interviewed his neighbours, had him in the police station, searched the shop and family rooms more than once for poison. They turned the whole man's life upside down and were coming close to exhuming the body when a new witness came forward to raise her suspicions against Mrs Greengage."

"Who was that?" Clara asked.

"A lady named Madame Delmont."

"Really? That's interesting."

"Now may I continue?" The inspector said tartly. "The police backed off as soon as they knew the truth. Mrs Greengage was in quite a predicament and had to admit that she had lied about witnessing the poison sales and had actually only heard about it via Lily.

"Lily Bundle had been quite talkative about her death apparently and visited Mrs Greengage nightly to talk about her awful demise and press the clairvoyant to do something. She claimed Ted had been poisoning her for months and the final dose had been left for her in her jar of coffee. She was the only one in the family who drank the stuff, so Ted was quite safe lacing it. If he did, of course.

"There was no evidence, however. No chemists recognised Mr Bundle and the coffee jar had been emptied long ago and reused for sugar, so even if the police believed Mrs Greengage, or should I say, Lily Bundle, there was no way of proving their suspicions.

"But public opinion can be dreadfully damning and Ted Bundle found a black cloud had been cast over him. His shop was ostracised by the locals, though the seasonal trade kept him going. He was shunned by former friends, was voted off the local shopkeeper's committee and in general became the least popular man in Eastbourne.

"It seems this, along with his real grief for Lily and the determined campaign Mrs Greengage kept up against him, finally tipped him over the edge.

"One night he thought he spotted a prowler outside as he was closing up. A sensible man would have just kept watch or called the police. Ted Bundle grabbed a carving knife from the kitchen and attacked the man. In the subsequent scuffle the suspected prowler was killed, stabbed repeatedly. Only then did Mr Bundle recognise the face of his prowler as that of a local policeman who was off duty at the time and awaiting his fiancée.

"You can imagine the outrage it caused. Bundle's only saving grace was that he was deemed insane. He'll spend the rest of his days in an asylum."

Park-Coombs stopped and took a long sip of tepid tea.

"What about Mrs Greengage?" Clara asked. "Surely someone must have seen her accusations as the spark that ignited Bundle's madness?"

"That they did. Her campaign of hate against Mr Bundle was used by his defence team as a reason for his insanity. Many people felt if she had kept her mouth shut the poor policeman wouldn't be dead," the inspector agreed. "Besides the murder of Lily Bundle had never been proved, many felt Mrs Greengage was a trouble maker, stirring up old dirt unnecessarily. Suddenly she was the one everyone disliked! I'm not surprised she had to leave Eastbourne."

"I see," Clara said, only she didn't 'see', not really. She had thought learning about the crime Mrs Greengage had become involved in would answer everything. Only it didn't, unless...

"Mr Bundle is in the asylum right now?"

"Yes, I checked," the inspector looked conspiratorial. "I don't mind admitting that we are at a dead end with this too. Mrs Wilton as the killer no longer makes sense and anyway, I don't think she is capable of murder."

"Exactly what I have been saying," Clara managed to keep the note of triumph out of her voice.

"I thought this Bundle case might give us some leads too. I have a worrying feeling this is going to be one of the cases we have to mark as unsolved."

Clara had that feeling too and it depressed her. Her first real case and she seemed set to fail. What would become of her reputation if she couldn't solve her one and only murder case? Thoughts of Mrs Wilton had long ago gone out the window; this case was about pride now. She had to solve it, she just had to!

Chapter Eighteen

T he headache was back and Clara rubbed at her temples
agitatedly. She was sitting at the dinner table with Tommy
again, after a weary day. She was still trying to pluck up the energy to
tell him about her feared 'pursuer'. She was concerned he would get
all silly and insist she didn't go out alone or something similar.

Fortunately her follower had not reappeared when she left the
inspector and she was able to persuade the young constable who
accompanied her home to leave her at the corner of the road, so
Tommy would not spot her escort. Still, she supposed it was only fair
to tell him.

"Tommy..."

"I did a little digging into Mr Greengage's past today," Tommy
interrupted her. "There are some quite interesting books on pre-war
theatricals and I found his name mentioned remarkably often. He was
rather famous in certain circles; apparently for a ventriloquist he was
quite exceptional."

"It's a shame he cannot be persuaded to perform again," Clara concurred. "He doesn't have a penny to his name. How he will ever get by I just don't know."

"War does funny things to people," Tommy said darkly, then he visibly brightened. "Something will come up for the old fellow, don't worry."

"I only wish I could figure out this murder and maybe bring him some peace that way."

"The funeral's tomorrow, isn't it?"

"Yes."

"Are you going?"

Clara groaned inwardly, the last thing she needed was a funeral.

"I don't think so."

"Could be a familiar face there? A new suspect?" His sister didn't reply so he decided not to push his luck. "I suppose we can definitely rule out Bundle as a possibility, presuming he really is in the mad house."

"Don't call it that," Clara said quietly.

"I was in one, so I am allowed to," Tommy winked at her, trying to lighten the mood.

"You were in a military hospital," Clara said firmly. She struggled to talk about that dark period in her sibling's life. "Anyway, the Inspector assured me Mr Bundle was still where he is supposed to be."

"What about the younger Bundles? The children?" Tommy pointed out. "Family seeking revenge on behalf of a loved one is as old as the Romans."

Clara considered this. How old would the Bundle's son be by now? Twenty? Could he be the man seen loitering around? Her pursuer? He looked older than twenty, but as Tommy said, war did funny things to people. He might just appear older than he actually was.

Yet the inspector seemed very certain that whoever this 'watcher' was he was unlikely to have been involved in the actual murder. Killers didn't linger around the crime scene usually. Though Clara knew as well as anyone else that people did not always do what was logical or sensible, and policemen were not always right.

"She let the killer in, I'm sure of that," Clara said aloud. "If one of the Bundle children turned up to talk she would probably ask them in. She might even feel bad enough about the fate of their father to not be suspicious of their late arrival."

"It's a possibility anyway," Tommy agreed. "Better than Mrs Wilton."

"The Inspector has come to his senses and ruled her out of the inquiries. He's not as pig-headed as I first thought. I suppose I will have to go see her."

The conversation was cut short as Annie entered with a rather small roasted chicken and some limp greens. At least there were plenty of potatoes. There were always plenty of potatoes.

"Not joining us for supper Annie?" Tommy asked when he saw they were lacking a third place setting.

"Oh, but I can't," Annie answered with a wink at Clara. "I'm off to the pictures."

"With whom?" Tommy achieved looking stunned and appalled at the same time.

"With Alice Roberts who works for Dr Macpherson."

Tommy turned to Clara agog.

"Who?" He seemed only mildly relieved it was not a young man.

"Alice Roberts," Clara told him sternly. "Honestly, men never listen! The maid who cleans at the Greengages' house and accidentally opened that bureau where the riddles were kept."

"I'm on a mission," Annie added proudly. "To interview Alice discreetly and get the 'scoop' on her."

"You've been reading my American detective books again," Tommy glared at the pair of them.

"I've got a nose for gossip," Annie tapped her nose and gave Clara another, more theatrical, wink before leaving the room.

"I suppose it was only a matter of time before you corrupted her too," Tommy shook his head at his sister. "Is Alice a suspect?"

"For the murder? Of course not!" Clara spoke confidently, but as soon as she said the words she had to reconsider. Was anyone excused from being a suspect? "My word, a maid could slip in poison so easily!"

Tommy looked alarmed.

"I was only jesting!"

"Whichever way you look at it poison is a woman's weapon, I'm afraid," Clara drummed her fingers on the table. "My mind keeps thinking of Lucrezia Borgia."

"Ah, but that's another matter. Lucrezia has been railroaded by history."

"Pardon?"

"Don't you remember your history? It was her father and brother who poisoned everyone, probably with arsenic by the way. The myth about Lucrezia being a serial poisoner came about much later."

"I've been so dense," Clara scolded herself. "I was so quick to take the incident with the poison at face value."

"And?"

"What if it is a red herring? Designed to throw us off the scent? Even perhaps to make us suspect a woman and make us turn away from wondering about the real murderer?"

"Who are you thinking of?"

"Maybe Mr Greengage tried to poison his wife and when that failed he shot her."

"But he has an alibi."

"For the shooting but not the poisoning."

"I'm not sure…"

"The poison had to come from someone in the house, didn't it?"

"Maybe," Tommy consented reluctantly. "But you, yourself, said about the maid being a possible suspect. What about other clients? It would only take a second to dose a glass of sherry."

"Except it wasn't in the sherry! Why didn't I see that before, just how was Augustus poisoned? No, the more I think about it the more I think the poison was meant to lead us astray. We both agreed that shooting and poisoning were two very different forms of murder, and it seemed unlikely that the same murderer committed both crimes, but what if it was meant to look like that?"

"Mr Greengage still has an alibi for the shooting."

"So he had an accomplice, why not?" Clara cast up her hands in triumph. Tommy remained dubious.

"What of motive? You said yourself that Mr Greengage is virtually destitute without his wife."

"One thing at a time," Clara almost snapped, not wanting this bubble to burst. "Tomorrow I will take a tour of the chemists of Brighton and see if anyone has sold strychnine to a man fitting Mr Greengage's description. They have to list all those sales in a poisons book, don't they?"

"The man doesn't leave his house!"

"So he says! But he managed to move from Eastbourne to here, what if he is merely trying to build up further proof of his lack of a motive?"

"Still… it will be a long job, do you know how many chemists there are in Brighton."

"Long job or not, it is real detective work. Didn't father used to have a trade directory somewhere?"

Clara was up from the table, her meal abandoned and rushing to her father's study to scour his books. Tommy sighed and helped himself to her potatoes.

Chapter Nineteen

Alice had promised to meet Annie at the entrance to the picture
house. There was more snow in the air and Annie stamped her
feet as she waited impatiently. Most of the other patrons were inside
and the picture would be starting any minute. She was starting to
wonder if Alice had seen through her invitation and changed her mind
when the girl appeared, running down the road.

"Sorry! Sorry!" She cried coming to a halt so fast she splattered
wet slush onto Annie's legs. "Dr Macpherson's surgery appointments
overran and there was such a lot of clearing up to do and the
charwoman who usually helps has her grandson down with the
measles."

"Well, I think we are in time to catch the start if we hurry."

They handed over their pennies at the ticket booth and found seats
in the half empty auditorium. It seemed colder inside the building and
the girls kept their coats on as their breath fogged before their faces.

"Have you seen this one?" Alice asked as the screen flickered into
life.

Annie didn't recognise the nondescript title.

"No."

"I've seen it twice, I love the pictures. It's a murder mystery. The girl did it," Alice gasped as she realised what she had said. "Golly, I'm terribly sorry! I do rattle off my mouth some times. Have I ruined it for you?"

Annie replied that she hadn't, while wondering how Clara could contemplate this girl as being a criminal of any description. She supposed it was possible she was a thief, the ditzy types could be prone to such vices Annie had found in her experience.

They watched the film for a while, Alice occasionally commenting in a manner that she probably considered helpful about important clues and the backgrounds of the characters. At one point a person in the next row shushed her.

"Golly!" Alice exclaimed in a whisper. "Some people are rude! Though... do you think I talk too much? Jeannette says I do."

"Jeannette?" Annie was utterly bored with the rather dull film that seemed to be building up to a mediocre climax.

"You know, that maid at Mrs Pembroke's house."

Annie pictured a young lady arguing over the price of a map.

"Oh yes, I recall her. I didn't realise she was a friend of yours."

"Well," Alice's jolly face fell, "I thought she was."

There was a long pause and then, in the tone of someone confiding an immense secret, Alice continued hurriedly.

"We used to come to the pictures all the time together. We met once at the home of that clairvoyant who died. I was cleaning and Jeannette had come for a reading."

Annie pricked up her ears; this was something Clara would want to know.

"I'm not sure how she afforded it, mind," Alice went on without waiting for a response. "Mrs Greengage wasn't cheap but I assumed she had money from a relative or something."

Alice was either very trusting or a confident liar, Annie concluded. *She* would have been immediately suspicious of Jeannette.

"Jeannette had to wait a while before the reading and we chatted. She was ever so lonely," Alice paused again. "At least, she said she was anyway. We talked a while and got quite chummy and then I said I liked the pictures and she said, so did she, but she didn't like going alone and not knowing anyone here meant she never went. So naturally I asked her to come with me. I don't really have a lot of friends, do you?"

"Not many," Annie admitted. "It's hard when you work like we do."

"Exactly!" Alice was clearly pleased to have found a kindred spirit. "Me and Jeannette went to the pictures quite a bit after that. Every day off I had, in fact. It was a little hard on my purse but Jeannette would insist on paying if I was short."

Annie wondered again at this girl's trusting nature.

"Do you ever think some people weren't meant to be maids?" Alice said thoughtfully. "Not me, of course! Heavens, no! All I know is scrubbing and cleaning. But Jeannette is different, I think her name sounds French, don't you?"

"Maybe. Different how?"

"She was ever so well spoken and educated. Knew all sorts of things and could do her sums like a... a... a... professor! She spoke a little French, that's why I wondered about her name."

"Perhaps her family had fallen on hard times and she had to work," Annie suggested.

"That's what I thought, but you can't ask people, can you?" Alice teased the finger of her glove. "It was all that money she had that worried me. After a while I started to think to myself, where do girls like us get that sort of money?"

That was a good question, and the only answers Annie could think of were all decidedly illegal. Yet she wasn't about to say that to Alice.

"Perhaps Mrs Pembroke is a generous employer."

"Hah! No fear! She keeps her claws firmly on her purse!" Alice spoke a little loud and someone shushed her again. Even in the darkness of the seats Annie knew the girl was blushing.

"Want to get a cup of tea?" She offered.

"Yes please. You won't mind missing the end?"

Annie indicated she wouldn't, in fact she had lost interest in the torturous plot some time ago. The girls retreated to across the road where a late-night café was serving teas and suppers. Annie paid 3d for a pot of tea and a cheese sandwich, while Alice fumbled in her purse and finally found a penny for her own pot of tea. They settled in a corner table by the big glass windows and watched fresh snow begin to fall.

"I hate snow," Alice gave a little shudder. "Dr Macpherson's patients are ever so inconsiderate and walk it all in on their shoes. His carpets are sodden by the end of the day."

Annie watched the clumps of flakes falling, trying to work out how to return the conversation to Jeannette. Fortunately Alice offered her an opening.

"I was quite surprised you inviting me to the flicks like this," the teas had just arrived and she was warming her hands on the brown teapot.

"I have been meaning to ask you for ages, but as we said work gets in the way and then I saw Jeannette and it reminded me," Annie answered.

"You saw Jeannette?"

"Yes, in the bookshop buying a map."

"A map?"

Annie was sure she wasn't just imagining the anxiety that suddenly came over Alice.

"You could hardly miss her," she continued. "She was making such a fuss. Whatever can she want a map of Brighton for? I ask myself. Do you know?"

"She can be quite cagey about things," Alice fiddled with her teaspoon. Annie decided to push her luck.

"I don't entirely trust her, you know. You mind she doesn't get you into any trouble."

The teaspoon clattered to the floor. Several customers glanced up, but Alice had her head in her hands and couldn't see them. Annie retrieved the spoon and slid it in front of her.

"Whatever is the matter, Alice?"

"You are so nice, Annie. So, so nice. If you knew what I had done, you would never speak to me again."

The cheese sandwich arrived at that moment. Annie took one half and slipped it onto Alice's saucer.

"Here, eat that. I didn't mean to upset you. I think you are a nice person too."

Slowly Alice put down her hands. After a moment she took the sandwich half and nibbled the corner.

"Thank you," she said quietly.

They ate and drank for a while in silence, and then Alice poured herself a second cup of tea and gave a sigh of resignation.

"I think I will tell you what I have done."

"Please don't feel it necessary," Annie replied, trying to mask her curiosity.

"No, I must tell someone because the guilt is eating me up and I keep thinking what would mother say? I did something awful,

Annie," tears sparkled in the girl's eyes.

Annie felt sorry for her, she looked so vulnerable and silly.

"Did Jeannette put you up to whatever it was?"

"Yes," Alice found her hanky and dabbed at her eyes. "She knew I worked at the Greengages' house once a week and she reckoned she had heard that there were these riddles to a hidden treasure in the house. She asked me to look when I cleaned. Honestly, Annie, I didn't like the idea of prying, but Jeannette said it wasn't that at all, it was just me keeping my eyes open."

Alice groaned.

"Yet in the end I did have to pry. Jeannette kept pushing me and telling me I was daft because I couldn't find them and I started to realise I was a little afraid of her."

Alice was pulling her hanky through her hands over and over.

"I didn't mean to open the bureau," Alice almost let out a sob with the confession. "I was only dusting really, and the catch was loose."

"Lying now won't make it better, Alice," Annie said carefully.

"You are right. So right. I opened the bureau on purpose," Alice's voice trembled a little. "And there they were, this little packet of riddles in an envelope."

"Did you take them?"

"No!" Alice was indignant. "I may have looked but I am no thief!"

Annie resisted smiling at the girl's strangely mixed standards.

"What did you do then?"

"Nothing. Didn't even read them. I did tell Jeannette though and she was really cross that I hadn't brought them to her. She thought I should have stole them for her."

"I hope you put her right, Alice. They aren't hers and she can't bully you into taking them for her," Annie found she was actually quite cross with Jeannette. She would have words with her next time she saw her.

"That's just the thing though, she did keep pushing me and then that awful day came and I didn't know what to do so I ran for Jeannette."

"You mean the day of the murder?"

"Yes. I was cleaning the Greengages' house that day. Mrs Greengage was a nice old bird, ever so strapped for money though. Often there was not even soap powder in the cupboard and she would tell me to just do the kitchen floor with a mop and water. It were ever so sad, but she refused to turn me away as she knew how I needed the money just as bad," Alice shook her head miserably. "Sometimes I snuck soap from Dr Macpherson's house, that weren't wrong, were it? I felt so sorry for her."

Annie touched her hand comfortingly.

"It must have been awful when she was found dead."

"It was. I found her! I came in at around eight, the back door was unlocked, which was usual. Mrs Greengage always used to be up and would unlock the door so I didn't have to knock and disturb Mr Greengage," Alice grew silent as the memory flooded back to her. "I always leave the front room to last, it usually only needs a good dust and the carpets beating, seeing as how little it is used. The door was a little ajar, which was odd as Mrs Greengage was thorough at closing things up before she goes to bed of a night. She couldn't stand a door left half open, it quite annoyed her. But there you are, I thought, we all have our bad days and forget ourselves.

"In I went and at first nothing seemed wrong. Someone had left the sherry glasses out but I was used to that and I went to pick them up to take to the kitchen. It was as I moved around the room that I saw her just lying there. I thought at first she had had a funny turn, the curtains were still drawn, you see, and they don't hold with turning the gas lights on during the day because of the cost. I opened the curtains and then I saw the blood.

"I was all at sixes and sevens over it. I weren't thinking straight else I would have run for the police, but all I kept thinking was how we found Uncle Billy like that during the war. Suicide, of course, because he couldn't face going back to the trenches, and I remember thinking what possible reason could Mrs Greengage have for killing herself? You see, it never occurred to me it was murder, so I suppose that's why I never thought of running to the police.

"Anyway, Mr Greengage was sleeping off his nightly tonic and he is always as bleary as a badger in daylight until mid-morning. So I hurried off to find Jeannette."

"Why her?" Annie asked.

"Well, she is the only other girl like me who I knew well and I couldn't rightly wake one of the neighbours. I suppose I could have fetched Dr Macpherson, but he would have expected payment for the call out and I doubt Mrs Greengage would have liked the expense, had she been able to know and anyway, Jeannette was nearer."

"What happened next?"

"Not a lot really. Jeannette said I should fetch the police so I did. Oh, and we woke Mr Greengage when I returned."

"Wait a moment," Annie held up her hand to halt the girl. "You left Jeannette alone in the house?"

"Yes."

Annie felt close to trying to shake some sense into the silly girl.

"Now why didn't you send *her* to fetch the police?"

"She... oh... Jeannette just, I suppose, sent me and I... I went."

Yes, thought Annie, little obedient, trusting Alice would not even pause to think when Jeannette told her to go. She would run off without hesitating, leaving Jeannette all alone downstairs and free to do as she pleased.

"Did you know those riddles in the bureau are missing?"

Alice looked stunned, clearly she didn't.

"You mean, Jeannette took them while I was gone?"

"It would seem so."

"Why?" Alice was tearful. "I mean, I know she wanted them, but to take them behind my back like that... I could have got in awful trouble with the police or Mr Greengage. I thought she was my friend."

Alice looked grief-stricken at the notion of being betrayed and Annie felt a pang of sympathy for her again. She poured her a third cup of tea from her own pot.

"I suggest you stay away from Jeannette."

"Yes," Alice said miserably, "I really thought she was my friend."

Annie patted her hand. It was getting late and the snow was lying thickly outside.

They parted company at the door and Annie watched Alice's slight figure vanishing into the darkness, before she set off for home concentrating on all the things she had to tell Clara.

Chapter Twenty

C lara's trawl of local chemists for sales of strychnine to a man fitting Mr Greengage's description had proved a dead end.

She stood in Harwoods and Sons, the last pharmacy she could reach by walking, and browsed forlornly through their 'sales of poison' book. It was useful that Mr Harwood was so amenable; he shouldn't have let her look at the book at all.

"Any good?" Mr Harwood, a man with outsized, old-fashioned sideburns, asked.

Clara shook her head.

"Try this one," Mr Harwood drew out another black bound book with 'poison' inscribed on its cover in gold. "It's my weekend book. I keep them separate on account of having different lads on at the weekend. It saves confusion when a matter like this arises."

Clara took the proffered book half-heartedly. She did not anticipate more success with weekend poisoners then the regular weekday ones.

"Was there any particular name you were looking for?" It was a quiet morning for Mr Harwood and his full attention was on his sole customer.

"Greengage," Clara said with a frown.

"Aha!" Harwood became excited. "11.21 am, Saturday, 12th

January."

He grabbed the book and flipped through rapidly.

"There we are, 'purchase of 5 grains strychnine.' I don't usually sell such small amounts and to be honest it was an estimate, I don't have a scale precise enough for such small doses. The lady only wanted a pinch – her words exactly."

Clara looked at the black ink entry in astonishment.

"Wanted it to deal with mice, she said. I told her she wanted more than a pinch to sort out a mouse infestation, the blighters can survive a good dose in my experience and there are always more of them than what you see," Harwood seemed aggrieved by the ignorance of some of his customers. "I said, 'You want a good packet of arsenic for mice' and, as God is my witness, she looked me square in the eyes and said she had been told strychnine was more humane! I said humane is not my business, effective is, and if she wanted rid of mice she was a fool not to take the arsenic. She wouldn't be swayed. I reckon she was one of those animal society people, the ones who call you a brute if you trip over the cat."

Clara stared at the entry while he spoke, trying to get the details into her head. Mr Greengage had not bought the poison, it had been his wife! That only raised new questions about the cause of Augustus' death.

"Would she have had some strychnine left over?" she asked.

"Didn't you hear what I said? It was barely a dose, it would have taken some doing to save some."

"Was it enough to kill a person?"

Harwood looked stunned.

"You don't think..." He shook his head. "A grain can be sufficient to kill an adult, but in most, ahem, murders a far larger amount is required due to the necessity of mixing the poison with something

– food or drink. Strychnine is very bitter and getting a person to eat enough can be tricky. I'm afraid as a chemist you do hear about these things. That's why we have the poisons book."

"You've been very helpful." Clara smiled at him and, as he had been so attentive, she added, "A box of aspirin please."

She would add it to the six other boxes in her bag that she had purchased during her inquiries, having felt rather mean to ask lots of questions of the various chemists in Brighton and then buy nothing. Well, at least she was well prepared should she have another headache.

Back out on the street Clara tried to see how this new puzzle piece fitted into the whole. Could it be Mrs Greengage had placed the poison in the sherry herself to make everyone think her life was in danger and then committed suicide? The inspector had ruled out suicide so quickly, but could he have been wrong? She retraced her steps, she had a call to pay on Mrs Wilton.

Mrs Wilton's worn down villa-style bungalow overlooked the sea and could have fetched a profit for the lady had she been inclined to sell. Clara wondered why she didn't, but then sentimentality was rarely logical. Mrs Wilton opened the door herself and gave a slight start at seeing Clara.

"Miss Fitzgerald! Elaine's up to her ears in laundry so I told her to stay put while I answered the door," Mrs, Wilton seemed flustered and the excuse lacked a ring of truth. Clara suspected Elaine rarely made it to the door to answer it.

"Come in," Mrs Wilton opened the door a fraction wider. "Do you have news?"

"Some," Clara admitted, stepping inside and easing off her gloves. She couldn't help but notice the hall was unswept and an ambitious spider had cast a large web across one corner of the ceiling.

"The parlour," Mrs Wilton conducted her guest out of the hall and into a room with a large sofa as quickly as she could.

The parlour was fresh and clean, recently swept and tidied. Clara might have attributed Elaine's neglect of the hall to over-work had she not spotted Mrs Wilton nudging an old rag duster under the sofa. She guessed who really did the cleaning.

"Elaine must have her hands full keeping this place running, especially with the sea breeze blowing sand and salt straight at you. I hear it can be quite a problem with seaside properties."

"She is very good," Mrs Wilton said, offering a seat on a decaying sofa. "Very understanding when money is a touch tight."

More likely irritated when her wages have been spent on séances and private investigators, Clara thought to herself as she sat on the sofa.

"I am sure you will be glad to know the police no longer consider you a suspect."

Mrs Wilton sighed and flopped back into a chair.

"That is a relief! I mean, I knew they could never really consider me... but one does worry so," she flapped a strand of hair from her face. "Do they have another suspect then?"

"Not yet, they've come to rather a dead end."

"Oh dear! And what about you?"

Clara took a moment to consider her response.

"I have some ideas in mind, which is part of the reason I came to visit you. You see, there is a little problem with your riddles."

"I was hoping you would mention them, oh, but a problem? Does

Mr Greengage want more money? He struck me as the grasping sort."

Mrs Wilton had a finger in her mouth and was chewing on it unconsciously.

"They have been stolen," Clara decided blunt was best. "However, I know who probably took them, I just need a bit more information before I accuse anyone."

"Gosh, you really are a real detective! Accusing someone! But who would steal my riddles?"

"Exactly, few people would understand their importance or know they could lead, possibly, to your late husband's hidden wealth."

"Not 'possibly', my dear, I trusted Mrs Greengage," Mrs Wilton pressed a finger to her lips. "So who knew except myself? That is a good question."

"Who have you told about the riddles?"

"Nobody!" Mrs Wilton was affronted, then she relented. "I mentioned them to Mrs Cole when we met in the lending library. She was very coarse about them and I did not care for her tone. I didn't say much to anyone after that, I mentioned I was seeing Mrs Greengage to some of my spiritualist friends, but no specifics."

"What about Elaine?"

"Elaine?" Mrs Wilton was now plucking at the edge of her lip. "I told her I was at the séances, yes, and I think I may have said in passing about the riddles."

"Could I talk to her?" Clara asked.

Mrs Wilton looked ruffled at the suggestion.

"Is it really necessary?"

Clara had the impression Mrs Wilton did not want another woman meeting her maid. It made her even more curious about the elusive Elaine and her relationship with her mistress.

"If you want the riddles back, I will need to speak to her."

Mrs Wilton sighed.

"You really put me in such a position. You won't be accusing her?"

"Don't be alarmed. I shall not be relieving you of your servant," Clara promised.

"She isn't much, but I really couldn't do without her," Mrs Wilton stood and pulled a cord near the fireplace that attached to an old bell pull. Somewhere in the depths of the house a bell could be heard tinkling. Clara noted that a modern buzzer bell was fixed to the wall beside the cord, but was clearly not working. It probably ran on electricity, which would be one luxury too far for Mrs Wilton these days.

It was several moments before Elaine appeared in the doorway. She didn't bother to curtsey, though it seemed from her rolled up sleeves and red hands that, at least, she had been genuinely doing the laundry.

"Miss," she said rather curtly and improperly.

"My visitor has some questions for you regarding the riddles Mrs Greengage gave me and which are now missing," Mrs Wilton explained crisply.

"I didn't steal 'em!" Elaine snapped, sending a vicious glare in Clara's direction.

Clara decided she didn't like this little harpy who seemed so quick to fill with spite and malice.

"I was not under the impression you had taken them," Clara said smartly.

"Oh? Well what do you want then?" Elaine folded her arms defensively over her chest, and Clara concluded that no servant at all would be better than employing this vixen.

"Do you remember the riddles?"

"I think I only briefly mentioned them," Mrs Wilton interrupted.

"Honestly, miss, forget your own head you will," Elaine bawled out, and her mistress looked abashed. "She showed 'em to me. They fell out of her bag, not surprising the times I've fixed the catch on it. It came open in the hall and these scraps of paper flew out. I thought they were nonsense rhymes, I like those, my Chad can do some good 'uns you know."

"Her young man," Mrs Wilton whispered in Clara's ear.

"I admit I read 'em and said to her," she pointed at Mrs Wilton, "'are these yours miss? Because they ain't much good and I should know as my Chad won a contest for best limerick at last summer's fair.'"

Elaine puffed up her chest with pride as she spoke of beloved Chad. Clara was already sick of him.

"Miss said they weren't rhymes but riddles and I said that didn't sound a barrel of laughs and she said, 'oh, but you don't know, Elaine, they lead to a treasure' and I said 'what a load of codswallop.'"

"Elaine does speak her mind," Mrs Wilton fluttered nervously.

"I'm honest, that's all, more than can be said for most girls in service, fawning to their ladies. Like your girl."

Clara realised the last statement was directed at her.

"Annie?" She said dumb-founded.

"Yes, she's a right one. Hearing her talk you would think you were the Queen of Sheba! She pinched me on the arm once for my saying it ain't fit a woman setting herself up in business as a detective. And you shouldn't be encouraging my mistress," Elaine pointed that finger again at Mrs Wilton.

Clara resolved to give Annie a hug as soon as she got home, and thanked her lucky stars she had her and not Elaine!

"It ain't fit," Elaine concluded.

"You must remember your manners, Elaine," Mrs Wilton clucked, utterly embarrassed by the indignant serving girl.

"Whatever you may think of me," Clara said sternly, "I hope you would have the decency not to shame your good mistress."

"Whatever can you mean, miss?" Elaine looked disconcerted, and Clara was pleased to see there was at least one way to take the wind out of her sails.

"Mrs Wilton's riddles have been stolen, and before you swear at me you 'ain't touched them,' I do not mean the ones in her handbag, but the ones that remained at Mrs Greengage's house. Now, I think I know who took them, but I need some information from you to confirm it," Clara felt back in control of the situation and Elaine had gone stonily quiet. "All I need to know is who you told about the riddles."

"No one!" Elaine burst out automatically.

Clara said nothing, waiting in silence until it was clear she expected a better answer.

"I mentioned 'em to Chad," Elaine finally admitted. "He don't believe in any treasure neither."

"But someone else did," persisted Clara.

Elaine's eyes went wide, taken aback that Clara should know all her business. She glanced at Mrs Wilton suspiciously, but she was fussing with her handkerchief.

"You don't know what it's like being a maid here on half the wages of the other girls and having to work for *her*," Elaine on the defensive was nastier than when she had merely been irritated.

"Don't say that. I'm good to you," Mrs Wilton flapped.

"They laugh at me, they do, for working for such a poor mistress, who talks all this nonsense about spirits and spends my wages on pathetic séances!"

"That only happened the once," Mrs Wilton sounded pitiful.

"It's all I can do to hold my head up when they are cackling at me."

"Who mocks you, Elaine?" Clara finally felt they were getting somewhere.

"Are you going to tell 'em?" Elaine suddenly appeared anxious.

"I have no reason to," Clara replied, "but I think you told them about the riddles, didn't you? When they were teasing, it just came out, yes?"

"They said I didn't have no prospects because I was as common as a fishwife and worked for Mrs Wilton only because she was too poor to hire anyone else. And I said, that's all you know, I have prospects, my mistress is coming into money and they said how? And I said she been talking to this clairvoyant who says Mr Wilton left a load of money hidden away, only he was afraid of burglars or robbers, you see, so he put the instructions to find the treasure in riddles. They still laughed, but later they thought better of it and were real chummy in case I did come into money. 'Cos, I've been good to my mistress and put up with a lot, so she was bound to reward me!"

Clara glanced at Mrs Wilton who had almost her entire fist wedged in her mouth, trying to bear the humiliation of hearing her maid talk like this.

"Who teased you Elaine?" Clara asked.

"That girl of Mrs Pembroke's. Jeannette. She is a real snob, though she is only a maid too, but she gets cast-offs from Mrs Pembroke, real nice stuff. And then there is that Alice Roberts who was always hanging around trying to befriend her. She would laugh along to please Jeannette though she had to bear many a joke at her expense too," Elaine paused, "Now I think about it, Jeannette started being real nice to Alice the same time she tried to pal up to me."

"So you told her all about the riddles."

"She kept asking and it was nice not being laughed at," Elaine scowled. "I didn't expect it to last or anything, but you don't know how it is and they were only stupid riddles."

"Thank you, Elaine, you've told me all I needed to know."

"You can get back to the laundry now," Mrs Wilton told her maid sharply.

Elaine shot a dark look at her and then retreated from the room.

"It is not true, you realise," Mrs Wilton said hastily to Clara. "She *is* well paid and provided for."

"I'm sure," Clara said soothingly. "Do not worry, I shall not take what she said about you seriously. Now, I should be on my way."

"Of course," Mrs Wilton jumped to her feet. "It was an error in my budget, you know, when I spent her wages on the séance."

Clara reached out and squeezed her hand.

"I understand."

They were at the door.

"I'm not good with money or servants," Mrs Wilton appeared close to tears. "When you get the riddles back, solve them for me, would you?"

Clara nodded and said her farewells. On the path she took a deep breath of sea air. It was bitterly cold and stung her face. She doubted she would make it home before dark.

Turning to head up the path she spotted *him* watching. She was still fired up from the interview with Elaine and she was tired of this stalking nonsense. Clara strode out purposefully towards him. Immediately he turned around and bolted. She quickened her pace, but when she reached the point in the road where he had stood he was gone, just like a ghost.

Chapter
Twenty-One

"I need to talk to you about something Tommy."

Clara was home. It was early evening and a small fire was burning in the grate of the old hearth. Tommy was busy at the table drawing out various tables of suspects, evidence and clues. He had been at it for hours and the result was quite impressive, even if the reams of paper made Clara feel all the more confused about the case.

"What about?" Tommy asked. "Here, do you suppose your information from the chemist counts as evidence or a clue?"

"It's evidence if she killed herself. Could she have killed herself, Tommy?"

"Don't know, old bean. You saw the body."

Clara shuddered at the thought.

"I don't know enough about guns to say, but that isn't what I wanted to talk about."

"What then?"

"I've had a spot of bother, I didn't want to say before and worry you, but now I think I should."

Tommy abruptly gave her his full attention, dropping the papers.

"You're worrying me, old girl."

"It's not that serious. A strange man has been following me, that is all."

"That is all!" Tommy said in horror. "Who is he?"

"I don't know, I told you he is a stranger. He turned up after I started to pursue this case. I first saw him at the Greengage's house, hovering in the street and then he appeared at Eastbourne. Next he was on a footpath when I left Mrs Wilton's house."

"Why didn't you tell me this? He could be the murderer!"

"Inspector Park-Coombs doesn't think so, says a murderer is smarter than that. Besides he is a bit like a startled rabbit, when I approached him he just bolted."

"You approached him?"

It was hard to picture Tommy looking any more horrified than he did right then.

"I was cross and as I say, he seems harmless."

Tommy slapped his forehead with his hand.

"Listen to yourself! From now on you mustn't go out alone, either myself or Annie will come with you."

"I knew you would say that," Clara moaned.

"It is the only logical thing to do! Normal people don't follow other people about."

Clara shook her head.

"I appreciate that, but it isn't really convenient."

"Keeping you safe isn't convenient?"

"You know what I mean," Clara was regretting bringing up the topic at all. "Besides, if Mrs Greengage killed herself there is no killer."

"That only makes your stalker more worrying."

Clara studiously ignored the comment.

"I am quite certain now that Mrs Greengage poisoned Augustus deliberately. The poison was such a small amount it could only have been for a very specific purpose. So was it a diversion to make us think she was murdered rather than that she had actually committed suicide?"

"It is possible."

"But why Tommy?" Clara felt the confusion returning.

"People have all sorts of reasons. To implicate someone else, maybe this Mr Bundle, or to cover up her own crime. She was religious and might have wanted to avoid the scandal in her church. Maybe she had life insurance."

"Mr Greengage hasn't mentioned it and he is now facing destitution, so he would want to get any insurance sorted if there was any. Whichever way you look at it, I am back to my Lucrezia Borgia theory."

"Except the Borgias used their 'skills' to get rid of people who were in the way."

"Augustus was a money-maker, it makes no sense to kill him," Clara idly picked up one of the papers Tommy had been working on and gazed at it blankly until the words blurred before her eyes.

"I think I will visit the Inspector tomorrow and have a word about Mrs Pembroke's maid."

"I'll come with you," Tommy said a tad too quickly and Clara's eyes flicked up at him.

"I need to go to the library," he added with a shrug. "And I would like to see those crime scene photos if you wouldn't mind."

"You are welcome to," Clara smiled. "And if we see my stalker I'll set you on him."

Tommy grinned.

"I could do with a bit of action in my life. How fast do you think

Annie can push me?"

"I will ensure you only encounter him when he is suitably downhill," Clara leaned over and kissed her brother on the cheek. "If only we could…"

"Don't say it old bean, I have to get used to it. I pray for a miracle, but I don't expect one."

Clara hugged him.

"You are far braver than me."

"Nonsense! You chase madmen who are stalking you!"

Clara laughed.

"That's different and don't ask me how, it just is."

Inspector Park-Coombs leaned forward on his desk.

"So Mrs Greengage bought the poison?"

"It seems so."

"And this Jeannette stole the riddles?"

"Will you arrest her?"

"We've had no report of a theft, as it stands she just took some bits of paper no one seemed bothered about. She could argue she thought they were rubbish."

"Most likely they are," Clara frowned. "I will deal with Jeannette then, if that is all right?"

"You are welcome to and I do appreciate you keeping us informed," the inspector paused then knotted his fingers together and stared at the fist he had made. "I confess when we first met I thought you were a bored busy-body."

Clara raised her eyebrows.

"Who says I am not?"

The inspector smiled.

"You have a knack for this business, a talent for sniffing out information. If you were a man I would want you on my force and be pushing you for detective."

"With due respect, I think I have more freedom in my inquiries than the average policeman and I would have to turn down the offer."

"It is a moot point anyway, what with you being a woman."

Clara's expression suggested she had already noted this.

"Still, I think the force is missing out, the woman's touch and all that. You are non-threatening and your casual methods seem to gain the confidence of certain witnesses."

"Meaning they deem a bored busy-body as no threat to them?" Clara asked defiantly.

"You take my words too seriously, but I have to say I have enjoyed our little chats on this case despite myself."

"Your tone seems to imply there won't be anymore?"

"The Greengage case is being put to one side," the inspector looked downcast. "Orders from above. There are no suspects and no real leads. It is a dead end and my superiors have other more promising cases which they want me to look into."

"I will apologise on Mrs Greengage's behalf that she could not be more promising," Clara snorted.

"It is a matter of logistics and resources. We have a royal visit proposed and my officers have to be drilled, and a bank robbery in Hove is taking up a lot of my time. I don't like dropping a case but when we are at a dead end like this and other matters call our attention we have to respond," the inspector rested his chin on his fisted hands, "Then again, I was rather hoping you would be inclined to pursue the matter as you have made such interesting progress already."

The inspector's eyes glittered mischievously.

"You want me to do your work for you?"

"Weren't you already?"

Clara feigned a scowl.

"Does this mean I am working for the police?"

"Not officially. It just means you are responding to a problem."

"And being a busy-body."

"If you like," the inspector became more serious. "And when you know who the murderer is come to me and I will arrest the blighter."

"You'll need evidence."

"I don't expect you to let me down on that front."

Clara sat back in her chair feeling she was being taken advantage of. It crossed her mind that when she pin-pointed the culprit it would be the inspector who would gain all the credit.

"Well, I am sure we both have a lot to do," the inspector politely dismissed her.

Clara took the hint and rose from her chair.

"By the way, almost forgot," the inspector paused her. "I made a few extra enquiries about Bundle. I thought it might be his son who was stalking you."

"Yes?"

"Master Bundle is in the Navy and serving abroad currently, so not our fellow, but it just sprang to mind, the daughter who found Mrs Bundle dead, her name was Jean."

Clara's mouth fell open in surprise, and then she grinned.

"In my experience criminals are rarely imaginative," the inspector added.

"My, my, the world is small and the Bundle connection was perhaps not so far-fetched," Clara reached for the door. "Goodbye, Inspector.

I have a maid to see about some riddles."

The inspector waved her a goodbye and then returned to his new cases with the hint of a smile still playing on his lips.

Chapter
Twenty-Two

"**O**liver Bankes?" Tommy held out his hand to the photographer. Annie had dropped him at the shop before heading for the butcher's. They had not been able to persuade Clara that she needed accompanying all the way to the police station, but had compromised at following her halfway. It just so happened halfway brought Tommy to Oliver Bankes' doorstep.

"How can I help you?" Oliver asked.

"I believe you know my sister, Clara?"

Oliver looked worried.

"Yes?"

"I'm helping her with the Greengage case and she is trying to rule out death by suicide and I thought I might take a look at the crime scene photos?"

A lady in a hat laden with false flowers and feathers looked up with a startled expression from the *Bankes' Photography Catalogue* she was browsing.

"I'm not really supposed to show them to anyone," Oliver

mumbled. "I allowed Clara to see them as a favour."

Tommy narrowed his eyes at him, understanding the implication and wondering the best way to turn it to his advantage.

"Have you heard about the stalker?" He said loud enough so that the lady customer now had her attention riveted on him.

"She did tell me, I thought the police were dealing with it," Oliver shifted his feet uncomfortably.

"Nothing much they can do, he turned up again yesterday."

"Is Clara all right?" Oliver bit his tongue at the quite obvious note of concern in his voice.

"She is fine. But if we could wrap up the Greengage case, then maybe we would have something to use against the stalker. I think it obvious he is connected."

Oliver glanced at his lady customer who was pretending to be absorbed by the Bankes' catalogue.

"You better come out the back," he sighed.

In Oliver's office the clutter Clara had first noted was still present and blissfully growing. Oliver scraped papers from a spare chair before clumsily realising Tommy didn't need it.

"Sorry," he said ashamed.

"No bother, you would be amazed how many people fail to notice. To be honest I would rather that than you fussing about me like a nursemaid."

"Good job my receptionist isn't here then, she fusses everyone like an invalid."

Tommy laughed and it broke the tension.

"I could probably make tea," Oliver dragged some cups from under a pile of papers and stared inside them as if that might achieve the result without having to fetch water and a kettle.

"I think I can survive without," Tommy assured him. "I just want to see the photos."

"Oh yes," Oliver dropped the cups back on the desk and went to a set of wooden filing cabinets that at least seemed well-maintained.

"From what I hear the police have given up hope on the matter," Oliver pulled out a cream coloured file. "It happens more often than you would think when they can't find an instant suspect. So many crimes involve spouses or lovers and the guilty party is caught red-handed. But there are some that just boggle the mind."

Oliver handed the file to Tommy and he withdrew several black and white photographs. The first happened to be a close-up of the dead Mrs Greengage and he hesitated.

"Did you know her?" Oliver asked.

"Only met her once," Tommy croaked, he had seen one too many dead bodies in his time, but they still shocked him with their cold, stillness. "How do you do it? Take their picture?"

Oliver shrugged.

"It doesn't bother me like that. I feel sad sometimes. I never get over seeing a person who has had their life snuffed from them. But I don't feel the shock some do." Oliver scrubbed at his nose. "My uncle was an undertaker. I saw a fair few bodies before I was even ten. I think it makes you more immune. It's not that it isn't still horrible, but you know that no more harm can come to them and you have a job to get on with. I think it helps not having much of an imagination too."

Tommy knew what he meant. Some of the men he had served with found nothing chilling about the death all around them. They could step over a corpse and not think about who it was or when they last spoke to them or whether it would be them next. Others, like himself, had to screw themselves up tight just to face the next moment, to bite down on the scream that wanted to obliterate them.

He purposefully put the close-up of Mrs Greengage face-down on the desk. The next shot was further away and at an angle that made it hard to see the features of the woman's face. Somehow that made it easier to look at.

"Did you say Clara has a theory of suicide?" Oliver asked. He was sitting in a wooden desk chair that swivelled and was twisting himself left and right with the toe of one foot.

"Sort of. Mrs Greengage bought the poison herself."

"Ah," Oliver let this sink in as he gazed at the ceiling. "And there was none in the sherry glasses?"

"No, but Clara's theory is all wrong. Mrs Greengage did not kill herself."

"Are you sure?" Oliver was out of his chair and looking over Tommy's shoulder.

"See the hole? It's near where you expect the heart to be, but a little low. To do that yourself you would have to hold your arm like this."

He demonstrated by taking Oliver's right arm and twisting it round until his hand pointed at his left breast.

"A pistol is about this long," Tommy gauged the distance Oliver's hand was from his heart. "Suicides don't want a mistake, so the muzzle will be pressed against you, or at least very close. You'll be shaking probably too, you'll need the gun steady not to make a mistake. Now pretend to pull the trigger."

Oliver mimed the moving of his forefinger pulling back on a pistol trigger.

"It's awkward," he noted.

"Yes. The boys in the trenches preferred a shot to the temple or a barrel in the mouth. For certainty," Tommy stared at the picture grimly. "Though I do remember one aiming for the heart like this. We always said that we thought he didn't really mean it and wanted someone to find him in time. But of course it would have done no good if we had saved him, he would have been court-martialled for attempting to get out of fighting. They would have shot him for desertion."

Tommy's eyes had taken on a glazed look. Oliver touched his shoulder lightly.

"I wasn't there, but I have heard," he licked his lips which were suddenly dry. "They reckon I have a bad heart and wouldn't let me in. I never could fathom if I was relieved or not."

"No one wants to fight," Tommy said.

"No, but no one wants to be left behind and called a coward either," Oliver returned to his chair. "Father felt it necessary to put a notice in the paper with the official medical report findings."

Tommy nodded. He had heard such stories before.

"So," Oliver came out of his thoughts. "Mrs Greengage could have shot herself but it would be awkward."

"Oh, no," Tommy seemed to wake up too. "You see when a gun barrel leans against you it leaves a mark when it fires, the soot and dust that come from the bullet shooting out, and sometimes burning because the explosive inside makes the chamber red hot. The skin and clothes get little scorch marks and there is lots of black powder. There is none of that on this woman. Her blouse is white. You would have noticed any marks."

He flicked through the photos and found a close shot of the bullet hole.

"See, the only marks are blood and the hole in her blouse is very neat and no burning."

Oliver examined the photo.

"Was Clara hopeful for suicide?"

"I doubt it, she would feel it was an anti-climax," Tommy shrugged. "But she is feeling quite stumped at the moment."

Tommy had come to some photographs of the table, and then some more of the rug the body lay on.

"I take all sorts of shots, you never know what the police will want," Oliver said apologetically as he caught Tommy looking at one vague photograph of the Indian-style floor rug. "They are always asking things like, 'Mr Bankes, have you a picture of that second painting on the wall from the right, perhaps with a small corner of the what-not cabinet to its left? I think it might be relevant to the case.' Oh yes, they come up with all sorts of ideas, so I cover myself and take everything."

"What is this by her hand?" Tommy pointed to a white speck on the rug, the edge of Mrs Greengage's arm could be seen near it.

"I have a close-up of her hands in that pile, is it better on that?"

Tommy filtered through the pile until he came to a zoomed in shot of Mrs Greengage's right hand. Lying close to the thumb seemed to be a button.

"Do you have a magnifying glass?"

Oliver disappeared to the corner of the room shuffling aside a potted plant to get to a bookcase. He returned with a magnifying glass on a wooden handle. Tommy took it without looking up and studied the small circle on the photo.

"Not a button," he noted. "A cufflink and, if I am not mistaken, a military one. The cheap sort shops sold before the war to give to men as leaving gifts, in case they had to go to a ceremonial dinner or something in dress uniform. Little did they know!"

He let Oliver take a look.

"The detail looks like a pair of flags crossed."

"Yes, the union jack and I believe the French flag. Later they did some with the America flag, when the Yanks finally decided to come out to play."

Oliver smirked.

"I bet those were popular."

"Well I wouldn't have worn them," Tommy grinned. "But I had a pair of these. My mother bought them. Last time I saw them was when our trench suddenly flooded in a storm and we had to get out with whatever we could carry."

"Is this a clue?" Oliver asked.

"Maybe," Tommy said. "It can't have belonged to Mrs Greengage."

"No, and she had no son that she might want to remember by holding on to them. So perhaps this fell off the killer?"

"If it did Clara is going to be all over Brighton asking about cufflinks," Tommy gave a mild groan and closed his eyes. "Worse, she may get me to do it."

"There must be hundreds of these things about."

"But few people still wear them. Most people are trying to forget the war," Tommy mused the problem. "And you don't dress up to kill someone, so whoever did it would normally wear cufflinks and these are perhaps his usual pair, so he never thought to take them off."

"He must have noticed they are missing by now."

"Yes, but does he know he lost one at the crime scene? When is the last time you could remember where you lost a cufflink or button?"

Oliver nodded at his office.

"In my life, never. I just buy a new pair."

"Ah!" Tommy grinned. "So we need to find who has bought cufflinks recently. Not a smart pair either, but a cheap work-a-day variety. And if they haven't had the time we need to look for someone who can't fasten their shirt cuffs."

"This is quite exciting!" Oliver smiled. "I never would have thought of all that from this little speck on a piece of paper. I told you I had no imagination."

"You don't think it far-fetched?"

"No, in fact, to prove it I shall blow up this photo and you can take a copy to Clara. It won't take a moment."

Oliver dashed out of the office and Tommy felt himself warming to the quirky photographer. He wondered how Clara got on with him; he suspected she might find him a little too clumsy and cluttered to suit her logical mind. She could never have worked in this office. Still, it took all sorts, and now he had a clue to take back to her. He was pretty pleased with himself.

Chapter Twenty-Three

Mrs Pembroke had one of the grand houses on Old Steine. She was old money and she was a snob. Her neighbours hardly knew her to speak to, she would not respond to their cheerful 'hallos' unless she had known their forefathers, and that those said forefathers had been of a social standing to equal her own. She didn't care for the modern world of up-and-coming businessmen who started life as barrow-boys and ended it in a smart house on the Old Steine. It was not fitting and she was finding that these days she barely knew anyone it was decent to talk to.

Mrs Pembroke was a widow and she lived alone, but she kept her home bustling with a host of servants that were another echo of the past. She did not need a parlourmaid and a housemaid, nor a housekeeper *and* a butler, but she had them because that was how things were supposed to be and if any of her neighbours grumbled that an aging widow had no call to keep a groom and a footman, when she no longer owned a carriage or horses, then she considered that merely because they were ignorant working-class plebeians who had fallen into a little money. And she ignored the fact that her groom spent most of his time drinking and gambling with the footman. As long as they looked the part and filled the regulation slot in her household she was happy.

No wonder, decided Clara, she had chosen a girl like Jeannette to replace her last housemaid.

"She came with fine recommendations," Mrs Pembroke said drinking from a china cup.

It had been difficult to get into the house; the Fitzgeralds had not been on a par with the Pembrokes at any stage in their existence, but Clara's father had once 'miraculously' cured Mrs Pembroke's lumbago problem and that had earned the family a position in the lady's affection that went against all her usual prejudices.

There was no point being old money and being able to make the rules, Mrs Pembroke contended, if you weren't also allowed to break them.

"I would not hire just anybody," Mrs Pembroke said with a sternness that suggested Clara was overstepping her mark.

"I have no concerns about Jeannette as a maid," Clara explained hastily. "I merely was under the impression that she may have seen something on the day of Mrs Greengage's death. She was friendly with Alice Roberts who occasionally cleaned at the house and I am told she helped on the day of the incident."

"Oh that little thing," Mrs Pembroke shrugged. "I never did have a lot of sympathy for those who dabbled with the dead, though it became quite the rage in the 80s and 90s. You could hardly go to a party without someone claiming to be a medium and starting up séances. It became quite dull. I never was inclined to speak to dear Mr Pembroke after he passed on. I found it quite impossible to imagine what I would say."

"I confess I am not much taken by this new spiritualist movement either," Clara said honestly.

Mrs Pembroke put down her cup and gave her an appraising look.

"Yes, you have the heart of your father beating inside you. A wonderful man," Mrs Pembroke suddenly reached out and touched Clara's hand, which seemed to indicate she approved of her. "He had a magical gift for medicine, wasted as a professor lecturing others I rather felt. I was sorry to hear of his death."

"It was a shock," Clara nodded. "He had such things in mind for when the war was over."

"Didn't we all," Mrs Pembroke drew back with a sigh. "I have to say I am surprised the police allowing a woman to investigate a murder. Oh don't get me wrong," she quickly added as she saw Clara about to speak, "I am not against you pursuing this. No, no, dear me, I was quite the suffragist in my time. In fact I drove dear Mr Pembroke quite potty with my talk of women's rights. He always thought me a silly thing, I fear, but here I am running his house comfortably enough. He seemed to make such a big deal of it, but really it is just a case of keeping good order and routine. I think men have underestimated us for too long you know. If I was a good deal younger I could quite imagine being a detective too, except it would mean talking to 'people'."

The term 'people' came out in a similar tone to one normally used for vermin and Clara assumed Mrs Pembroke referred to anyone beneath her own social status with the word.

"I suppose you wish to see her now," Mrs Pembroke drained her tea and put the cup and saucer down with a clatter. "I am to attend a lunchtime lecture at the Pavilion, I'm afraid. It is the price of being a patron to the arts, one must show one's face. I believe this one is about that silly abstract movement that is on the rise in painting, personally if anyone asked me to sponsor an exhibition of such monstrosities I would ask them to kindly walk off the end of the pier and not bother me further. But there, I suppose life must change and the young must have their novelties."

Clara politely nodded, uncertain what the correct response to this tirade should be.

"If you don't mind I will send you to the housekeeper's room for the interview. I would not want all my servants gossiping that I left a stranger unattended in my parlour."

"Quite," Clara nodded politely.

Mrs Pembroke was on her feet and ringing for a maid.

"I don't expect to come home and find I am missing a housemaid," she said coolly as the sound of the bell rang down the corridor.

"Of course not!" Clara feigned surprise and just hoped she could find some tactful way to call Jeannette a thief.

A maid appeared at the door and performed a deep curtsey.

"Take Miss Fitzgerald to the housekeeper's room and have Jeannette see her. She is having trouble with another maid and needs to speak to her," Mrs Pembroke instructed the girl, then she turned to Clara. "I doubt you will be here on my return so I will bid you a good day and do give my regards to your brother Timmy."

"Tommy."

"Indeed, lost his arms didn't he?"

"No just the use of his legs."

Mrs Pembroke looked puzzled.

"Who am I thinking of then?"

Clara gaped for an answer, but fortunately the clock was chiming, and Mrs Pembroke forgot her blunder to fuss about being late, and hurried out the door to find her waiting footman who had managed to hire a carriage for her. Clara watched her vanish out the door and marvelled at the Victorian relic of a woman who disappeared into the vehicle.

The maid bobbed another curtsey at her and led her down a long corridor into the depths of the house. They went down some stairs and she was in the basement world of the Pembroke servants, another relic of a long dead past. She could not imagine many Brighton households who would feel the need to keep so many servants, especially as most seemed idle, fussing with mundane tasks of little importance because there was nothing else to do.

"In here, miss."

Another corridor and Clara found herself being ushered into a well-appointed housekeeper's sitting room with a neat fireplace, a worn but tidy armchair and a folding table. The clatter of footsteps outside suggested she was standing at the front of the house again, though this time below street level, with a window placed high up to cast in daylight. She listened to people milling about in the snow slush outside until she heard the door open with a slight click and she turned.

"Jeannette Brown?" Clara asked as a girl peered around the door.

Jeannette nodded and entered. She was a proud looking creature with dark hair scraped back into a hard bun and strong features that could almost be described as manly. She was sharp-eyed, but she held her chin too high as if she wanted to look down on the world all the time and the line of her mouth made her look hard.

"Would you care to sit?" Clara asked.

Jeannette pulled a chair from near the folding table, a simple straight-backed wooden one, but still refused to sit down until Clara had nestled in the armchair. Clara was beginning to see why Mrs Pembroke liked her.

"I am here on behalf of a client to investigate the murder of Mrs Greengage. I believe you went to the house on the day the body was found?"

"Client?" Jeannette asked curiously.

"I am a private detective. You have heard of such people?"

"In American crime novels," Jeannette shrugged. "I didn't know women could do that."

"Women can do anything," Clara said stoutly, "if they set their mind to it."

She wondered if that hit a cord because for an instant Jeannette dropped her gaze. But it was swiftly back on her.

"Why do you want to talk to me?"

"You helped Alice Roberts."

"She is a useless creature," Jeannette answered and couldn't disguise a note of dislike. "She couldn't find her head in the dark."

"I thought you were her friend?"

Jeannette hesitated seeing she had stumbled.

"I was. Before I knew her well."

Clara took a breath, wondering how to broach the next topic. Jeannette was all bristles and bitterness, and she knew the slightest misstep would have her leaving in indignation.

"Has she said something against me?" Jeannette had interpreted the pause as a cue for her to continue talking. She had stumbled again.

"Why should she say anything against you?"

"She's jealous, because I work here and she doesn't," Jeannette had clutched her hands together and was pulling at her fingers unconsciously. "She hates me, I think."

Chapter Twenty-Four

"Now on that I think you are wrong, but really I am only interested in what happened that day."

"Alice came and fetched me," Jeannette said simply. "Came to the back door and asked for me. I was busy cleaning a grate, but she waited for me. She still had her hands dripping wet from getting ready to wash the floors at the Greengage's, her sleeves were rolled back and she hadn't a coat or shawl on. I told her she would catch her death and she said I had to come quickly. Well I did because she looked so bemused and upset. We got to the house and there was Mrs Greengage dead on the floor. She wanted me to go in and make sure she was a goner, but I said I wasn't moving and she should fetch the master of the house. She refused, said he liked to sleep in because of this medicine he takes and he wouldn't hear her if she knocked. So I said go get the police and let them wake him. That's what she did and I waited in the house for her."

"In which room?" Clara asked.

"Pardon miss?"

"In which room did you wait?"

"The hallway of course, I had no right being anywhere else. I only meant to be there in case Mr Greengage came downstairs and stumbled over his own dead wife."

Clara felt certain Jeannette seemed defensive and decided she could risk pushing her.

"I'm sure you will be relieved to know that no one thinks Alice had any hand in the death of her mistress."

"I never thought she did."

"Well, some suspicion arose because of the peculiar circumstance of the open bureau."

Jeannette paled slightly.

"What can you mean?"

"Oh, you know how police are. They see suspicion anywhere and they had this silly theory that someone had killed Mrs Greengage to get at her bureau where she was keeping some odd little riddles for one of her clients. The riddles are missing you see, and they supposedly lead to a treasure."

"Oh."

"Of course, no one can use them because there are nine riddles in total and only six were in the desk."

Jeannette was looking rather sick. Clara let the news sink in for a moment.

"Rather a risk you took for an incomplete set of riddles Jean Bundle."

Jeannette snapped up her head.

"My surname's Brown and please do not shorten my Christian name."

"All right," Clara sat back in her chair. "Mr Greengage has not reported the theft, so this is just between you and me, though be aware that the Inspector knows who took the riddles and will act if he feels he has cause. All I want is the riddles you stole back for their rightful owner."

"I didn't steal anything!" Jeannette cried out.

"Keep your voice down, someone will hear," Clara said. "You know how servants gossip and the last thing a maid needs is the word 'steal' associated with her name."

"I just waited in the house," Jeannette said in a steadier voice. "Waited with that dead corpse. I didn't want to do it."

"But Mrs Greengage had made a martyr of your father and it was rather satisfying looking at her body and thinking someone had had the guts to kill her," Clara said coldly.

"It wasn't like that," Jeannette shook her head. "I would never wish harm like that on anyone."

"She destroyed your father."

"Not alone she didn't!" Jeannette gulped, knowing she had come too far to turn back. "All of Eastbourne was against him. She might have started it, but they helped her along. People turned their backs on him, supposed friends. Our shop was always empty. Mother had a weak heart, we all knew it, the doctor came regularly, but no one would listen, not once that woman had set her mind to tearing us apart."

Jeannette shuddered on the verge of tears, the hardness in her face evaporating to be replaced by such an acute look of vulnerability that Clara felt infinitely sorry for her.

"If it is any consolation, I think what Mrs Greengage did concerning your mother's death was unspeakably horrid."

"She was a charlatan. Everyone knew it," Jeannette paused. "Well, everyone with sense knew it. There were others who thought different. She set her heart on ruining my father and I still don't understand why."

"You never had dealings with her?" Clara asked.

"No, none. She never came to the shop. Do you know why she did it?"

Clara cast down her eyes, she couldn't quite meet the girl's sad face.

"If I am honest I think it was purely a matter of convenience. I think she believed it might boost her business. She was a performer and she knew that scandal sold."

"You mean, she drove father almost mad, not to mention the rest of us, so she could get some publicity?"

Clara hesitated. Was that what she was saying? Did she really believe that? Unfortunately she did, she couldn't imagine Mrs Greengage pausing for one second to consider the misery she would inflict on the Bundles. She knew how to manipulate grief to her own advantage. Look how she had been intent on using Mrs Wilton; such callousness knew few limits.

"Yes, I fear that was what drove her."

Jeannette let out a ragged breath.

"She was evil then," she said.

"Perhaps, or just foolish. Does that mean she deserved to die?"

Jeannette pursed her lips and refused to comment. Clara doubted she could offer more than the expression on her face already told her.

"The riddles are another stunt. I have no qualms in telling you they are a load of nonsense dreamed up by Mrs Greengage to trick a foolish and desperate woman out of her money," Clara explained. "I presume you heard about them from Elaine, Mrs Wilton's maid."

"Yes," Jeannette said quietly. "Elaine thought they were a hoax too, but Elaine is rather a..." Jeannette looked about her for inspiration for an adjective that would sum up her feelings politely, "Sour individual. She can't see good in anything and despite my father I did know that some of the things Mrs Greengage said were true. She told old Mrs

Cole where she had lost her favourite hatpin and she predicted to the hour the flood that would ruin the vestry of Reverend Higgins' church. I thought she might be right this time too and it crossed my mind that it would be fitting if that treasure she had found came to me who she had so hurt. I didn't think about Mrs Wilton."

"Hatred can be as blinding as love," Clara shrugged. "I presume you won't mind returning the riddles. They do belong to Mrs Wilton after all."

Jeannette nodded and asked Clara to wait. She was gone a moment and then returned with a small, worn purse. She unclipped it and handed over the riddles.

"Thank you."

"I couldn't understand them anyway," Jeannette shook her head. "I even got a map of Brighton! But it made no difference, waste of 5d."

Clara didn't mention that she had already heard the tale of the map.

"May I ask why you came to Brighton in the first place? It was to pursue Mrs Greengage, wasn't it?"

Jeannette bought some time fiddling with the clasp on her purse and then twisted her hands together.

"I think I did want revenge. My father is locked up now, did you know?"

"I did."

"His nerves had been shot to pieces after what Mrs Greengage had done. The police had been at our door, poking around the shop, someone said they would exhume mother," Jeannette grimaced. "I thought it would finish me, I really did. I felt like giving up, only father and my brother and sisters held me together. I thought father was being so strong and when we heard that the police knew Mrs Greengage was lying we thought it would all come right. But they wouldn't do anything, said she was just mad and it would be a waste of their time to prosecute her for being a nuisance.

"I think that did it. Father was shattered and the shop was close to ruin. He was barely sleeping and I caught him crying a few times. He loved mother and it tore him up inside to hear people saying he had murdered her for her money, it was horrible.

"And then one evening he saw this man outside. There had been trouble with lads throwing rocks at the windows and dabbing paint on our door, he had sworn the next time he spotted them trying it he would beat some sense into them. So he saw this man and... I suppose... he just snapped inside," Jeannette trembled. "I didn't see it. Only found him afterwards with the knife in his hand. He was staring at the man he had killed and said he was done for. They would have hung him had they not declared him insane."

"Where did they send him?" Clara asked.

"Broadmoor," Jeannette bit her lip. "That's bad enough isn't it?"

"And you came looking for Mrs Greengage."

"I didn't kill her," Jeannette broke into sobs. "I wanted to talk to her, maybe make her feel bad for what she had done, but I could never pluck up the courage and then I heard about the riddles... I wanted to hurt her like she hurt us, make her know what it was like to have people's spite turned at you. But how could she feel that if she were dead? No, I wanted her alive to suffer."

Jeannette pulled a cotton handkerchief from her sleeve and wiped at her eyes.

"I understand," And Clara did, she knew what it was like to feel hurt and pain, and to want to reflect it back on the ones who had caused the torment in the first place. "I only have one last question. Did you come alone to Brighton?"

"Oh. Yes," Jeannette looked puzzled. "Why?"

"A young man has been seen wandering around and no one knows who he is, someone suggested he could be connected to the Bundle family?"

"I only have a brother, Alfie, and he went to sea," Jeannette put away her hanky, her emotions back under her control. "Alfie went to sea, Katie got married and Susan took over the shop. People seem to think you should give up when something like this has happened, but we moved on. I came here and found Mrs Pembroke. I suppose you guessed the references were forged?"

"I did wonder how you had had the time to be a maid when you were helping your father."

"Will you tell?"

Clara shook her head.

"Mrs Pembroke is very satisfied with you and I see no reason to spoil that. References do not maketh the maid!" Clara smiled at her own joke. "She made me swear I wouldn't scare you off before I was allowed to speak to you."

"That is good to know," Jeannette looked calmer. "I am actually quite happy here as Jeannette Brown."

She gave Clara a meaningful look.

"I won't tell a soul who you really are," Clara promised.

"Now the riddles are back the police won't bother me?"

"They have no reason to."

Jeannette sighed with relief.

"I wish Mrs Wilton better luck with them than I had."

"They are a wild goose chase," Clara answered firmly. "But hope keeps people going."

"Well I best show you out and get back to work," Jeannette stood and straightened her skirt. "I hope you find who did this, I genuinely do."

Clara found that now Jeannette had let her guard down she was actually quite likeable, she allowed her to escort her to the front door.

"One last thing," Clara said as she was on the doorstep. "I am aware you befriended Alice Roberts because of her employment with Mrs Greengage."

Jeannette looked guilty.

"As wrong as those intentions were it would be a shame not to continue a friendship which had proved agreeable."

"Alice is rather a mouse," Jeannette gave an awkward smile. "But she is a nice girl."

"And lonely," Clara added, "She doesn't deserve to be misused because of Mrs Greengage either."

"I'll put it right," Jeannette nodded. "I'm making a new life for myself here and I need to forget what has happened in the past."

Clara bid her farewell, feeling that another little part of the world was put to rights. It was only when she reached the pavement that the realisation she had yet to find the real killer of Mrs Greengage dampened her optimism.

Chapter
Twenty-Five

T ommy toyed with the scraps of paper on the table. It was after dinner and they were drinking tea in the parlour while mulling over the case. Clara was re-reading the handwritten report Tommy had worked on about the odd cufflink in the photo. He was a stickler for keeping evidence and clues in order and, above all else, writing them down so they could not be forgotten. Clara had gone over the report three times and now just sat staring at it, her eyes glazed and not really focused on the words.

"I think this one means a church," Tommy broke her out of her thoughts. "'House of sorrows, house of joy, turn to the east and follow the boy.' I think boy means Jesus and churches usually face east and they are places of happiness and sadness."

"Do you know how many churches there are in Brighton?" Clara replied.

"Perhaps when I figure out the others it will become obvious which church it means."

"You seem to be thinking that those notes mean anything. They are just gibberish."

"Mrs Greengage must have expected Mrs Wilton to solve them at some point."

Clara raised her eyebrows.

"You have met Mrs Wilton?"

Tommy shook his head.

"Look at this one, 'An oriental dream, or nightmare? Tread lightly on this spot, for Mr Fitzherbert is here.' That must mean the pavilion, Prince George had it built and he was madly in love with that Fitzherbert woman, even married her. He could be Mr Fitzherbert."

"Except men do not inherit their wives' names."

Tommy grumbled and shuffled the notes into one pile.

"You know, you can be quite infuriating!"

"I didn't write them!" Clara laughed.

"What of the cufflink, do you like that?"

"I agree that it is a clue," Clara nodded. "Perhaps not the easiest one, but it will be worth exploring."

"At least I can do something right," Tommy grinned. "Now about that Bankes fellow."

"What about him?" Clara asked casually, her eyes back on the paper.

Tommy paused and found his words faltering.

"He's a good... contact for a private detective to have."

"Oh definitely," Clara sighed and massaged her temples, a habit that Tommy had noticed her doing a lot lately. "Now, what must I do tomorrow? Ah yes, see Mrs Wilton about the riddles and visit Mr Greengage yet again."

"I intend to solve these riddles if it kills me. I have made copies."

"I am quite certain it will drive you insane. Oh I suppose I should visit the local jewellers and see if anyone has bought new cufflinks too.

Bother, Mr Greengage will have to wait."

"I don't think he is going anywhere," Tommy grinned.

"Poor man," Clara shook her head. "He is quite lost without his wife."

"It strikes me they were an unlikely partnership," Tommy rearranged the riddles before him. "I wonder what he was like before the war? His wife seems to have dominated him."

"That's unfair, he was obviously a nervous wreck and she had to take charge."

"By framing a man for murder?"

"That is rather sad," Clara admitted. "Mrs Greengage was rather ruthless, but then perhaps ruthlessness is born out of desperation."

"Let's hope not," Tommy replied. "Else the world will get a lot grimmer soon."

Clara pulled a face.

"Oh well, tomorrow is another day."

"They said in the newspapers more snow," Tommy glanced out the window at the night-time darkness. "Maybe you will have to curtail your investigations until the weather settles."

"Honestly Tommy, you believe whatever that paper tells you."

But he was right. Clara awoke to not only a drift of thick snow running up to the back door of the house but more snow falling heavily. She groaned as she dressed and wondered if the Brighton jewellers would have the courage to open today.

"You still determined to go out, old thing?" Tommy called to her as he was propelled by Annie into the dining room.

"Time waits for no man," Clara sighed.

"Does it wait for a woman though?" Tommy grinned at her. "Well, apparently I am housebound, snow disagrees with the old wheels."

He tapped the wheels of the chair.

"Doctor's orders."

He tilted his head to Annie.

"Tommy Fitzgerald you are the worst patient I have ever known!" Annie snapped with mock ferocity. "You gripe and groan like an ungrateful child."

"Thank you, dear," Tommy winked at her.

Annie blushed furiously and marched off to sort out the breakfast things.

"You shouldn't be so atrociously awful," Clara reprimanded him.

"Are you referring to me or the weather? Old bean, it is not fit weather for a dog to put a foot outside let alone a person."

Clara stood at the tall bay window of the dining room that overlooked the street and noted the lack of people about on their usual tasks. The snow was thinner on the roads, but even so no one had braved it, any horse and cart that tried would be forced to plough their way through, and she dreaded to think what it would do to any car that was driven in it. But Clara hated being put off a task almost as much as she hated being wrong.

"I say, Tommy, you'll have to take that back, why I see Mr Donald's mongrel out there right now attempting to find the gatepost to mark."

"I said it was not fit, not that dogs – or certain people – had the sense to recognise that," Tommy shook his head. "If I weren't a crock I would escort you..."

"Let's not start that again," Clara interrupted, turning briefly from the window. "You are far from a crock Tommy and I won't hear such talk."

She turned back to the window so she didn't have to see his scowl.

"What's this? Why we have a policeman heading to the door, Tommy, it seems Inspector Park-Coombs doesn't hold with snow either."

The heavy old Victorian bell rang, its spring rustling seconds before the clang, and alerting Annie before the chime had stopped. She glanced in the open dining room door as she went past.

"It's a policeman, Annie, you can let him in here," Clara called out.

Annie opened the door, spoke quietly to a person on the step and then led a cold looking policeman into the dining room. He didn't look very old and was shivering slightly after his long walk to the house. Clearly no one had suggested he cover his uniform with a greatcoat in case he was mistaken for an ordinary citizen, even if it did cost them a constable to pneumonia.

"Come stand by the fire and warm yourself," Clara offered as soon as she saw him.

"Thank you miss, sorry to be calling so early like," the constable touched the peak of his helmet in deference and then pulled it off with a popping sound before heading to the fireplace. A look of relief filled his face as he felt the warmth glowing over him.

"So, why has the Inspector got you running about town on a day like this?" Clara asked, perching herself near the fire.

"He thinks he might have something important for you. Two builders stumbled over a body this morning on the way to a house they are repairing. Looks like a tramp who was caught out last night and died in the cold. Inspector says the description sounds much like the man who was following you."

"Really?" Said Tommy wheeling a little closer.

"Man about thirty, short dark hair, greatcoat. No identity papers or money," the constable screwed up his eyes as he remembered what he had been told. "Terrible thing, freezing to death."

Tommy glanced at his sister. She was staring into space, her expression oddly neutral and her skin pale.

"Inspector wants you to come take a look. No rush though, they are still trying to get him back to the station. He was frozen solid to the ground. They have been getting the ladies nearby to boil kettles of water, but you can imagine what it is like in this weather," the constable nodded at the snow out the window and tutted as if it was particularly inconsiderate to die in such conditions. "When I was sent here, they was just about done. But plenty of time for a cup of tea like."

Clara woke from her daydream in time to catch the hint.

"Oh yes, would you care for a cup constable? I haven't eaten breakfast yet, so I am sure we could arrange some toast too?"

"Much obliged," the constable went to touch the peak of his helmet again and looked abashed when it wasn't there.

Annie disappeared with a queer look on her face to fix extra rations and Tommy motioned the constable to the table.

"Poor soul," Clara said as she carelessly slipped into her chair. "I had come to the conclusion there was no harm in him."

"He was stalking you!" Tommy sputtered.

"The gentleman's right," the constable added. "Sorts like that can't be trusted, they have something not right in the head, else why would they be following a lady about? It's not logical, no, best you not be fretting about it."

Clara scowled at his patronizing tone but the constable was too busy surveying the dining room to notice. Tommy did however and thought it best to move on the subject.

"I imagine this weather has the police busy?"

"Indeed sir. Pipes burst everywhere and carts getting stuck. We tell people if you have to deliver something do it on foot, the horses just can't pull in this weather. But they don't listen and tell us it's their livelihood and what do we know? Well I don't suppose we know a lot about it, but I know how many stuck carts I see in a day. No they always think it shan't be them, that *their* cart will make it through."

Annie returned with a warm pot of tea and an extra cup for the constable.

"I've set your coat before the fire to take a little warmth before you set out," she told Clara.

"You're very thoughtful, Annie," Clara noted how formal her friend was being before the constable, she wondered what had upset her. She wouldn't even look the man in the face.

"I'll go get the toast," Annie said and disappeared.

"We've had three deaths this morning as well," the constable continued sloshing milk and tea into his cup. "Including your tramp, there was a porter at the station dropped down dead. We think his heart couldn't take the cold, and an old lady in Church Street was found dead in a chair by a neighbour. But that isn't suspicious either, people drop like flies this time of year."

Clara was becoming irritated with the constable's light-hearted air as he talked about death. She was relieved to see Annie bring in the toast and to think she could get the morning's identification procedure over and done with soon. She had lost some of her appetite because of the news. Whatever Tommy and the constable said she hated to think of anyone having to sleep on the road and to die in the snow. She was certain her stalker had not been evil-minded, he seemed more frightened and anxious. If only he would have stopped and talked to her, but she supposed the encounter with Oliver had spooked him and he had feared she would call someone to see him off. Perhaps if they had spoken...

But it was all over now and who he was and what he wanted she would never know. She picked up a slice of toast knowing her two watchdogs, Tommy and Annie, would note how much she had eaten and Annie especially would be cross if she thought Clara had gone out with no food inside her. She was the sort of person that deemed no drama too big as to prevent a person having three square meals a day. In contrast to Clara's sluggish appetite, the constable had munched through his toast in seconds and was helping himself to another cup of tea.

"I shall escort you to the station as soon as I have drunk this, miss," he said as he noticed Clara rising. She wondered when he had suddenly decided that he gave orders to her? She headed for the kitchen for her coat and to get away for a moment or two from the annoying constable.

The kitchen, Annie's domain, was so warm it was hard to think of snow outdoors. The range was burning furiously and Annie was spitting on an iron to check its temperature as Clara walked in.

"I came for my coat," Clara said in response to Annie's look. "You don't think much of the constable do you?"

"You know who he is?"

"No."

"Name's Alfie Ling and if ever there is a fellow who should not be wearing a copper's uniform it is him," Annie sounded quite angry and slammed her heated iron down on an unfortunate piece of bed linen.

"What has he done to you?"

"What hasn't he done, more like? He grew up in the same road as me. Little toe-rag from the moment he could walk. My father gave him a hiding more than once for throwing stones at our cat and breaking the glass roof of the greenhouse. Any trouble in the street you could bet Alfie Ling was behind it. Windows broken, paint on doors, plants ripped up, bicycle wheels stolen. His mother was a night-owl, if you know what I mean."

Clara thought she did and decided not to ask for clarification.

"So he made it into the police?" Clara mused.

"Don't trust him whatever you do," Annie shook her head. "He has his fingers in those same old pies uniform or no uniform. You mark my words. He'll be trouble for them, and probably trouble for us too."

"He has no reason to bother us," Clara shrugged on her coat.

"He does if you carry on with the detecting and keep in with Inspector Park-Coombs. There's a man Ling can't pull the wool over. He's holding him back I've heard and Ling is bitter about it and he takes his bitterness out on anyone who is handy."

"I'll watch myself," Clara promised, determined no local bully would get the better of her.

"I know you will," Annie said, deflating a little. "I still feel like throttling him on sight for all the trouble he caused us. Did you see how he walked straight in with his wet boots?"

Annie looked quite forlorn at the thought of her stained carpets. Clara squeezed her shoulder.

"I think it's high time Mr Alfie Ling left my house."

Clara marched back down the hall to find Ling on his third cup of tea and finishing off the toast she had left on her plate. He was telling some amusing story that involved a great deal of laughter on his part, causing crumbs to spit over Tommy.

"Constable, I am ready to view your tramp," Clara said sternly.

"I'll just finish my tea, miss, no rush," Ling said, raising his cup to her.

Clara narrowed her eyes.

"Constable, you may have little work to amuse you today but I have a full diary and viewing a body was not on it until now. I wish to get this over and done with and I will head for the station whether you are with me or not." Clara marched for the door.

Ling looked astonished for a second, even Tommy was impressed with how scary his sister could sound. As the front door opened with a loud snap, Ling half dropped his cup and leapt to his feet.

"If the Inspector thinks I let her go alone I'll be high and dry!" He squeaked, grabbing his helmet and racing for the door.

Annie appeared at the dining room door as he legged it outside. She was looking quite satisfied with herself, Tommy noted, and didn't seem at all put out that Ling forgot to close the door behind him.

"Clara get stung or something?" Tommy asked, still reeling at the change in his sister.

"Good riddance, Alfie Ling," Annie said to no one, still smirking at the door.

Tommy shook his head. Women, he thought. Then he caught a scent of something in the air. He glanced at Annie.

"Can you smell burning cloth?"

Chapter Twenty-Six

C lara's last visit to a morgue had been under the sad circumstances of her parents' deaths. They had died in London and been identified by papers her father was carrying, but she still had to make a visit to the Capital to identify them formally before the bodies could be released for burial. No one had ever imagined the Germans would take out their wrath on London using ghastly silver Zeppelins that floated silently across the night sky. Sometimes just the memory of them had woken Clara from her sleep in a cold sweat. She would be forever grateful she had not been one of the unfortunates who had lost all their loved ones in the conflict; at least she still had Tommy.

Brighton's morgue smelt of disinfectant and bleach. It was kept cold by being partially underground and after the winter snowfall the white tiles on the wall were icy to the touch. Clara watched her breath fog before her face as she made her way down some stairs and was greeted by the head coroner.

"Miss Fitzgerald," he said offering a hand to shake. He made no mention of Alfie Ling who was hovering at the foot of the stairs. "I'm sorry to call you out on such an appalling morning."

"No matter, Mr...?"

"Deeth, Dr Deeth, only spelt D..E..A..T..H. It quite amuses some people but it is an old, old name. All my ancestors have been involved in medicine in some way." Dr Deáth was a pleasant man, not very tall and a little portly with black-rimmed, circular glasses propped on his snub nose making him look like an affable owl. Clara found herself liking him almost instantly. He seemed quite jolly for a man who worked around corpses all day long.

"Care to come into the crypt?" He asked. "My little joke, you'll see what I mean."

He led her down a cold corridor and around a corner until they reached a brown door. When he opened it Clara did understand what he meant. It seemed someone had been inspired to use ecclesiastical architecture in the construction of the morgue and the white room before them had a vaulted ceiling and pillars ranged along the walls. Big windows at one end allowed in some street light, but the rest of the room was lit by great swinging bulbs in green shades.

"I always feel rather holy in here!" Dr Deáth laughed. "I did have an uncle who wanted to become a priest, but they thought the name might cause awkwardness at funerals. He became an undertaker instead."

"Do you feel your surname has affected your job prospects at all, Dr Death?" Clara asked curiously, stepping into the sparkling white, empty room.

"Oh, no!" Dr Deáth smiled briskly. "I have one maiden aunt who's a midwife."

He brought forward a wooden chair and offered it to her. Clara sat, though would have rather remained standing, she had just noticed the rows of closed, small doors on the side wall and was beginning to have a nasty suspicion about what they were for.

"Just wait here and I will get our man," Dr Deáth scurried away, thankfully through a low arch and to some distant room. Clara relaxed again trying not to think there were rows of dead bodies just behind those cupboard doors.

When Deáth returned he was wheeling a recalcitrant table trolley, a similar thing to what Clara remembered from her hospital days. One wheel was jammed and kept catching on everything it went past.

"I didn't put him with the rest," Dr Deáth waved a hand at the ominous cupboards. "He was frozen solid and I needed him to thaw a little before I could examine him properly, so he has been resting in the staff tearoom."

Clara looked mildly stunned.

"Oh don't worry, I'm the only soul in today and he doesn't bother me," Dr Deáth grinned. "Would you care to take a look, I haven't touched him yet."

Clara stood from her chair reluctantly and took a pace forward. The body was covered with a white sheet and all she could make out were the contours of the poor man's body. She hesitated as she drew level with his sheet-covered head.

"How does he look?" She asked anxiously.

"Like he's asleep," Dr Deáth assured her. "Many victims that freeze to death, like our tramp here, fall into a doze first, often helped by alcohol and then don't notice the temperature dropping. Compared to some methods, I think it must be quite painless."

Clara wasn't sure that made her feel better.

"Are you ready to see him?"

Clara nodded, biting hard into her lower lip. Dr Deáth swooshed back the sheet from the corpse's head like a magician with a magic trick. For a second Clara's eyes refused to focus on the face, then slowly she controlled herself and took a good look. She let out a sigh.

"It's not him," she said.

Dr Deáth looked disappointed.

"What a shame, at least that would have been some sort of recognition. I guess this is another soul I have to list as 'unknown identity'."

Now her eyes had adjusted to the stranger's face, and she knew it was nobody she recognised, Clara found herself drawn to look at the poor man. He was the same age, roughly, as her stalker, had the same crop of brown hair, but his face was narrow and the lines harder. He looked weather-worn, as though he had been used to the outdoors and there was still a faint line where his neck and face were slightly darker than his pale shoulders and chest. He had once had a good tan.

"He is just a nobody?" Clara asked sadly.

Dr Deáth shrugged.

"Another tramp, we get plenty of them, especially this time of year. Probably an ex-soldier," Dr Deáth looked grim. "I find it depressing how many of them come through here, all fine lads who have been torn apart by conflict. I see far too many suicides."

Clara's mind flashed to Tommy. Then she blocked the thought out.

"I'm sorry I couldn't be more help."

"Never mind, I'll show you out."

They were coming to the morgue door when Clara had a spark of inspiration.

"Dr Deáth, did you autopsy Mrs Greengage?"

"Indeed I did."

"Could I ask, what did you find? I have been working with Inspector Park-Coombs on the matter as an outside investigator."

Dr Deáth shuffled his feet and looked uncomfortable.

"I'm not supposed to talk about my work."

"You could send Alfie Ling to get authority from the Inspector, but it is the honest truth. The Inspector has come to a dead end and I am pursuing matters that, for various reasons, he cannot."

Dr Deáth seemed rather twitchy.

"No one has ever asked me about an autopsy before."

"I wouldn't now if it wasn't important."

Dr Deáth rocked on his heels, his indecision palpable then he made the error of looking into Clara's eyes and he was caught, with a groan he knew he would get no peace if he didn't help.

"Perhaps you best come in the staffroom so no–one can over hear."

Clara wondered if he was referring to the morgue's dead inmates who might resent being handed to a man who shared their secrets.

The staff tea room was compact with a small fireplace, currently full of smouldering logs, a battered table and several worn armchairs. Dr Deáth offered to make tea as he was rather cold and Clara decided he would be more talkative if he felt this was a casual conversation, so she agreed. Eyeing a display skeleton of a person propped up one corner wearing a bowler hat and scarf (which she suspected belonged to Dr Death) she took a seat in a chair and waited as the kettle boiled.

Dr Deáth brought the filled teapot over to them wrapped in a green knitted cosy, and perched it by the fireplace before gathering two mugs.

"So..." he mused as he took the armchair beside Clara, "Mrs Greengage."

"What can you tell me about her death?"

"Well, it was somewhere between midnight and eight in the morning when the maid arrived. Single bullet to the chest, penetrating the heart and killing her near instantly. Gun wasn't more than three feet away, I would say."

"Which seems to confirm it was someone she knew and who she had let in."

"I told the police all that," Dr Death shrugged again. "No signs of a struggle or a fight, no defensive wounds. I would say she knew the person well enough, yes."

"Could you tell if the person was a good shot?"

Dr Deáth looked puzzled.

"What, in case it was luck they hit her heart? I don't think I can make that guess really, but it would have been a fairly simple shot from the distance I stated. Chest is the largest target anyway and you are bound to do damage."

Clara realised she was getting no further and was disappointed.

"Would there have been much noise?"

"Yes, bit like a loud 'pop'. I can't say if she made a noise, like a scream, of course."

"No, but I would guess she didn't as the police had no witnesses who heard a scream," Clara decided she was at a dead end again. "Well, never mind."

She drank her tea feeling the need to warm up before leaving and facing the cold again. She hoped Alfie Ling was standing on the steps freezing.

"If only Mr Greengage had not taken his sleeping draught, he would have been the prime witness."

"In my experience," Dr Deáth said between gulps of tea, "there is no legal sleeping draught a doctor can make that can send you into that heavy a sleep without some rather nasty side effects."

"Really?"

"My father's uncle was a chemist back in the day when you could mix up pretty much whatever you wanted. He had some fine concoctions, a lot were opium based, only he had to be careful who he sold to, because long term users started to hallucinate or suffer severe headaches. Some struggled to shake off the draught when they came to and others began to complain of aches and pains, especially in the bowels. One lady was particularly susceptible to the stuff and fell asleep for two days. Of course, I dare say prescriptions are better prepared these days."

"Mr Greengage seems to imply he has been on the sleeping draughts for years."

"Well, they won't be opium-based ones then, else he would be showing some severe side-effects."

"He seemed to rouse quite quickly when his wife was found dead and I have seen no sign of headaches," Clara was getting that feeling of puzzle pieces falling into place again. "How long does a sleeping draught last?"

"Depends on dosage, but eight to twelve hours roughly. Though the gentler ones mean the patient can still be disturbed from their slumber."

"The maid came in around eight as usual, we were there until around eight or nine the night before," Clara was working timings out. "It's all very close and Alice said Mr Greengage was never awake when she did her work, so how come he proved so awake that morning?"

"He was disturbed, perhaps the girl screamed?"

"No, she didn't," the thoughts in Clara's mind went click. "And even if it was a scream that woke him that means he was lying about taking a draught that would render him unable to hear his wife arguing with a visitor or being shot."

Clara jumped from her chair.

"Do excuse me, Dr Deáth, I must pay a call on the Inspector. You have been most helpful and the tea was lovely."

Dr Deáth smiled at her as she scurried out of his 'crypt'.

"I would say visit again, but it sounds rather morbid," he called. "I did enjoy our chat!"

Clara found Alfie Ling puffing on a cigarette and rubbing his hands at the foot of the stairs.

"Took your time, didn't you?" He grumbled as she approached.

Clara astutely ignored him.

"I have a call to make on the Inspector, Constable Ling," she said heading up the stairs. "And I have a feeling you may be having to wait out in the cold a lot longer before the day is done."

Swearing under his breath Alfie Ling followed her outside.

Chapter Twenty-Seven

Clara was beginning to develop a soft spot for chemists, they were very helpful people. Mr Palmer was an ample man who ran his little concern on the corner of North Street with the assistance of his wife and two unmarried daughters. He was deeply fascinated by the properties of the drugs he sold and it wasn't hard to get him into a lengthy conversation about any of his products. He was a walking pharmaceutical encyclopaedia and very content with his work. Perhaps his only downfall was his obvious inability for discretion.

"Mr Greengage? My word, I have been preparing his powders for months, I have." Mr Palmer was the sort of person who liked to be helpful and the mild enquiry about sleeping draughts mentioned to her by a friend had opened an entire dialogue. "Didn't recognise the doctor's name who prescribed them, he was up in Eastbourne anyway. But I took the prescription and filled it as needs be."

"And the powders are safe to be taken long-term?"

"Safe as houses, madam, all my goods are," Mr Palmer waved a hand at his stocked shelves. "I wouldn't care to sell a product which I thought harmful in any way. I won't even sell poisons, unless by special request and even then not to women or children."

That would explain why Mrs Greengage had not used her regular chemist for her strychnine dose.

"Are there any side-effects?" Clara pressed. "I have heard some bad reports about opium-based draughts."

"Not a drop of opium in the stuff, madam. Mild as a little lamb. Mostly herbs actually, dash of camomile, that sort of thing. It's a recipe from the Continent I do believe, but doctors favour it because it isn't addictive like the stronger drugs and doesn't have all the side-effects.

"But it works still?"

"Would I sell it to you if it didn't?" Mr Palmer laughed. "I tell ladies it is harmless enough to feed to teething babes, but good enough to take you to sleep when you need it."

"What worries me," Clara continued, giving every appearance of being a plaintive customer, "is that on occasion my brother has nightmares and gets quite distressed – the war, you see. And our maid always comes and wakes me to soothe him, I would hate to take something that would make that impossible."

"Madam, this powder is to get you asleep, but it don't imprison you there like some. Heavens, I would hate to be that dead to the world! I know some people like the strong stuff, but I think you can go too far. The maid will have no issues rousing you. The draught is more for relaxing you, really."

Clara nodded, examining the box he had produced for her with 'Cartwright's Patent Sleeping Doses' listed on the front.

"May I take two, to try?" She asked.

"Of course, madam, but I have never heard of them upsetting anyone." Mr Palmer carefully wrapped two twists of paper in an extra sheet and handed them to her. "That will be thruppence."

Clara fished through her purse for the money and then left with her purchase. Alfie Ling was standing outside waiting for her.

"Quite done?" He said, trying to coax some life back into his numb fingers.

"Nearly." Clara smiled at him. "The Inspector did say to do what I told you, remember."

"I don't think the Inspector thought I would be standing outside all day." Ling moaned.

Clara resisted the temptation to say the inspector had thought of it all right and been amused by the idea, but they were marching briskly to the Greengage residence and she didn't want to give him an opportunity to argue.

"You will have to wait around the corner until I am inside," Clara told him sternly. "I just want a quiet chat with Mr Greengage. Come back in a little while and listen at the door, I will shout if I need you."

Ling protested, but it was clear he could not win and he slumped off up the road looking aggrieved with the world and the frozen tramp who had put him in this mess in the first place.

Clara rapped on the door with her knuckles, discovering the door knocker was too frozen to move. She heard a shuffling inside and then someone coming to the door. After a moment it was opened.

"Hello Mr Greengage, how are you?" Clara put on her best 'concerned' expression, the sort she would use when at her desk and trying to look sympathetic to a client.

Mr Greengage took a moment to recognise her.

"Oh, Miss Fitzgerald, you came out in this?" His eyes drifted to the high banks of snow still lining the road.

"Unfortunately I had to be out in it anyway, so as I was passing I decided to do my Christian duty and check upon you. Now, how have you been?"

"Well... You know," Mr Greengage fumbled with his knitted waistcoat, Clara noted it was stained with splashes of a brown substance and had a slightly stale smell, "I did notice the kitchen was beginning to look a mess."

Clara chose to ignore that comment. If he expected her to start tidying the kitchen when he was perfectly able to do it himself he could think again.

"Why don't I come in for a little chat?" Clara tried to pretend the cold snow was not eating into her feet. "I brought a small gift."

She held up the wrapped parcel. Mr Greengage motioned her in, though he looked even more dazed and bemused than normal and seemed to be stumbling about the house in a fog, his mind elsewhere. Clara wondered if he had found some opium-based drug after all, but she supposed that was far-fetched and besides he never left the house if he could help it.

He almost motioned her into the front parlour, but Clara hastily found her way to the back study.

It seemed Mr Greengage had been doing most of his living in that room since she had last visited, if the untidy nature of the chairs and tables, the piled papers and numerous stacks of dirty plates were anything to go by.

"I see you are eating." Clara lifted a dish containing the remains of a beef stew from a chair and settled herself down.

"All the ladies in the road have been cooking for me." Mr. Greengage looked slightly helpless in the cluttered room, everything seemed to tower over him. "None of them have the time to clean though. I really need someone to do that."

"You could try for yourself," Clara suggested sweetly.

Mr Greengage gave her a look of horror.

"Oh, Martha would never allow that!" He said.

"Well, whatever the case. It had been on my mind that you might be having trouble sleeping with everything and I knew you took sleeping draughts, but perhaps had not been able to fetch them yourself. So I made a trip to Mr Palmer, the chemist and – I do hope you don't mind – but I made some enquiries and bought you these." She placed the parcel on a low table and unfolded it carefully.

Mr Greengage's eyes lit up as he saw the little twists of paper.

"You have no idea, dear lady, how you have saved my sanity." Mr Greengage took the sachets with such care they might have been made of gold. "I have not slept a wink since my powders ran out. I just can't seem to clear my mind and switch off."

"I would be quite happy to get more, if they are the right type?"

"Perfect, dear Miss Fitzgerald, perfect." Mr Greengage looked at her through watery eyes. "I haven't slept since the war. The trenches did it for me. The doctor in Eastbourne suggested these powders as they could be used forever without causing a problem. I had tried some of those quack remedies before, bought straight off a shelf and they had made me quite queer. I couldn't seem to wake up in the morning and my head would pound for hours. They brought me no peace, you know."

Mr Greengage stood and very carefully secreted the packets into the bureau. He looked quite relieved when he turned the key on a little drawer and locked his precious powders away. Clara watched him with a sinking feeling. He looked so benign and a little hopeless. He had lost everything with the loss of his wife and she was here not for the generous purposes she had asserted, but on a secret mission of subterfuge to catch a killer.

He returned to his chair and sat opposite her again.

"Thank you again." He held out his hand for her to shake and she instantly noted the loose cuffs.

"Do you normally wear cufflinks, Mr Greengage?" she said, taking his hand. "My father thought them the mark of a well-bred man."

Mr Greengage smiled at the veiled compliment.

"Indeed I do, but I have had the misfortune of misplacing one half of the pair I normally wear. My other cufflinks are simply too flashy for everyday use, I had them for on stage you see. A bit of sparkle in the act, dear Martha used to say."

Clara stared at the empty holes in the cuffs where a cufflink should be.

"My brother had a rather fine pair," she said, feeling sick as she spoke. "Someone bought them for him before he went into the military. Dear me, if I can't quite remember what they looked like. I meant to find them up and see if they would be any use to someone. Tommy refuses to wear them now, reminds him, you see. If I recall they had flags on them."

"Sounds like mine, they were a gift too. British and French flag flying on them," Mr Greengage said. "Martha got them just before I went to the Front, said I could use them at fancy dinners. Funny, but I was rather fond of them despite what they represented. I suppose because it was the last gift she gave me. After the war we were just too poor. Here, I'll show you the one I have left."

Mr Greengage went back to the bureau and poked about in drawers for a few moments, before returning with a small, silver, button-like object in his hand. He gave it to Clara. She held it in her palm with her heart sinking. There were the crossed flags identical to the two on the cufflink in the photo Tommy had seen. Everything was falling into place and she wished it wasn't. She looked into Mr. Greengage's open and smiling face and tried to kid herself that he couldn't have done it.

"Do you remember where you last had the other cufflink? I find retracing my steps helps?"

"Why, well it must be about a week ago. I never had them on when I went across the road on the day…" He stumbled, then regained his control. "It was commented upon that I had one missing and I was mortified. I was so glad to get back here so I could find the missing one, but you know I couldn't see it anywhere."

"I think I know where it is." Clara reached into her purse and drew out a scrap of tissue paper, carefully she unfolded it and set it beside its pair.

Chapter Twenty-Eight

"Wherever did you find that?" Mr Greengage said in surprise.

"The police had it among the other evidence for your wife's murder. The inspector was gracious enough to allow me to borrow it, you see, it was a bit of a dead end for them. It could have come from one of your wife's guests, for instance, though they hoped it belonged to the killer." Clara sighed. "They never considered you Mr Greengage. They believed the story about the sleeping draughts and no one could think of a motive, if anything you are dreadfully worse off without your wife."

Mr Greengage was staring at the cufflinks.

"I don't understand," he said.

"Yes, you do, Mr Greengage." Clara felt as though she was about to kick a lame dog. "Your alibi Mr Greengage simply does not work. The sleeping draughts you take are not strong enough to prevent you from being roused by a loud noise. A gun shot is a loud noise, and I cannot believe that Mrs. Greengage did not cry out when she saw the intruder, unless she knew there was no one to cry out to. And then there was what you told me about the maid, Alice, 'she didn't even scream', you said. How could you know that if you were asleep as you claimed? And you roused yourself pretty fast when the police were on their way, not the actions of a man who takes strong sleeping draughts."

Mr Greengage had picked up a cufflink and was fiddling with it in his hand. He was beginning to tremble.

"If you must know…" He began, then had to quell his shaking. "I heard the cry and the shot, but I was too scared to go look in case he got me too. I am a coward!"

"He? Mr Greengage?"

"The intruder. I was a coward in the war and Martha called me a coward from time to time when I began to get so I couldn't go on a stage. On that night I heard her open the door and call out, but I never moved. It was like being back in the trenches again and the bang seemed so unreal. I never thought no more about it, the house went quiet, and in the morning she was dead." Mr Greengage shifted the cufflink from hand to hand, his lips trembling ever so slightly, and a faint glistening tear trickling down his cheek.

"I almost believe you," Clara said stiffly, "Except your cufflink was left in the front parlour where *you*, Mr. Greengage, killed your wife."

"No." Mr Greengage shook his head.

"There is no one else. All the other suspects have been ruled out."

"There was the man in Eastbourne."

"He is in prison," Clara explained. "His son is away with the Navy. There is no one who could have done it, Mr Greengage, except you. I just don't understand why."

"Someone tried to poison my wife," Mr Greengage said sharply.

"She bought the poison herself, I discovered that, how it got into Augustus I don't know. But it was luck it only killed a parrot."

"Only a parrot!" Mr Greengage muttered, rocking slightly, then he turned his bleak eyes on Clara and blurted out. "Augustus meant the world to me and *she* killed him!"

Clara sensed they were closing on the truth, but she couldn't let Mr. Greengage falter his way there in a rage. Kindly she reached out and squeezed his hand.

"It's time to tell me everything so we can sort this mess out," she said softly, in a tone she remembered a kind teacher had once used towards her. She didn't feel she could blame the poor man, something had driven him to this dreadful situation and now he needed confession if he was to have any peace. He would send himself insane if not.

"Tell me about it."

"You saw Augustus, didn't you?" Mr Greengage had more tears in his eyes. "He was a fine bird. I bought him from a Sikh in London. He knew all sorts of things and with a little patience I had taught him to flap his wings on command and to pick up cards. He was amazing in my shows, pulled in the audiences and of course I always did his voice."

Greengage looked wistful.

"I thought the world of that bird, he travelled the country with me. It always struck me there was a sort of wisdom in his eyes. I had other animals too, but with Augustus it was different, you felt he understood you when you talked." He shuddered. "I dreaded leaving him during the war, I was not cut out for fighting and I did try and stay on at the music halls, but business was bad and Martha said it was not fit a healthy man shirking his duty. Besides, Augustus was white, and she said it looked rather dubious a man performing instead of fighting with all those white feathers about him."

Clara patted his hand.

"Many men felt the same," she assured him.

"I know, but I am a coward, always have been. Martha pushed me on and, as long as she was at my side, I could do anything. But once I was in France I was all alone and people were dying and all you could hear were bangs and men screaming." Mr. Greengage drew back his hands and pressed them against his ears for a moment while his eyes screwed up painfully and he seemed to be remembering the noise.

Gently Clara pulled his hands away.

"Let's not think of that. What about after the war, when you were home?"

"I was all wrong in the head." Mr Greengage's throat rattled with unvoiced sobs. "I got home and I just couldn't leave the house. I tried to go back to performing, Martha had booked some theatres and that first night I got myself all dressed up and Augustus was dusted with chalk to make his feathers glow and I got to the front door and I just couldn't move.

"My heart was pounding and my ears popping. The world seemed to sway and I could hear my own breathing as loud as a bell. I thought I was going to drop to the floor and put Augustus down sharply. Martha was furious, but I couldn't help it. She tried to get me out the house, oh she tried, but the first step I took out the door I sank to my knees and began weeping, so she swept me up and got me inside before the neighbours could see.

"That was it. My career was over. Martha marched off to the theatre to tell them I was ill and I returned to my bedroom with Augustus. Martha didn't understand, she had never felt like that, she was always strong and knew what to do. She had never been scared in her life and I knew she despised me at that moment, I felt it. She detested me because I wouldn't work and she could see no reason for it. Only Augustus understood. I could see it in his eyes as he sat beside me. He knew it wasn't my fault."

Clara slowly rubbed his hand as Mr Greengage finally descended into tears. He had suppressed himself for so long that now his emotions came out in a torrent.

"I understand," Clara promised. "The war changed people, and you are not a coward because of that. What happened to you is not so uncommon and things can be done to improve it, but you have to take it slowly."

"You are kind." Mr Greengage nodded. "You have been ever so kind, which is why I feel so awful..."

He pulled away from her.

"You are right, I did shoot my wife."

Clara fell back in her chair almost astonished by the confession; she had known but at the same time not wanted to know. She had expected him not to admit it, and without a confession, the inspector said nothing could be done. But he had spoken and so now she knew, and how she hated being right.

"Why Mr Greengage? Because she was a bully?"

"Oh no!" Mr Greengage looked appalled. "Martha was many things, but not that. We were poor, Miss Fitzgerald, but we tried to keep up appearances, before the war my performances kept us from starving. Martha always put rent before food because she knew how important it was for us to look respectable. I had to keep getting work, sometimes she would refuse to eat dinner so I could have a bigger meal, because she said I was the one that needed it.

"And then, when I came back from the Front... Once Martha realised I was not playing a fool and my head problems were real, she was very kind and started the medium business again and had me do the ventriloquism. She was a good woman, my Martha."

"Then why on earth did you kill her?" Clara couldn't hide her confusion. Was he really saying he loved this woman so much and then shot her?

"I never held a grudge, never, and I always forgave her foibles, but... but..." Mr Greengage sobbed, "she never should have done for Augustus! He was my bird, my f...friend."

Clara paused.

"The strychnine? It wasn't an accident, but it also wasn't to kill Mrs Greengage, it was always destined for Augustus."

"She must have put it in his seed. I knew what had happened when I saw him dead like that." Mr Greengage let a spasm of anger flicker over his face. "Martha had been on and on at me that he was sick and had to be dealt with. I told her to leave well alone, Augustus was a wise old bird and would tell me if he was unwell with a sign. She said I was blind to it and the bird was suffering, she called me cruel. I shouted take him to a vet then and she said, what makes you think we can afford a vet? No, best thing out is to put him out of his misery.'"

"She might have been right," Clara said tentatively. "Wasn't he quite old?"

"Don't say that! Not for a parrot!" Mr Greengage cried. "He kept me sane, that bird. I fed him from my own plate every night. He was just a bit peaky. He never did like the cold. But Martha would keep going on and on. She said she would get me another bird, a canary. I said how can I have a canary with its brainless warblings when I have had the pleasure of owning the king of birds? She said, how about a budgie then?"

"Are you saying...?"

"On the night he died, when you had all gone I confronted her and asked her what she had done. She said the bird was sick, she had told me before. But I knew there was something else, I knew. I said Martha what have you done? She couldn't lie anymore then." Mr Greengage suddenly looked very serious and a darkness had crept over his face.

"She said she couldn't bear to see the bird suffer anymore and she had done for him with strychnine. I felt like my heart had been ripped out. It was a betrayal beyond any I have ever suffered. I never argued with my wife, it was a principle, so I left the room with her trying to explain and saying she was sorry."

"And then later you came back and shot her," Clara said, her sympathy slowly fading. "Because of a parrot."

"Because of Augustus!" Mr Greengage yelled violently, and at the same moment there was a thud as the front door burst open and Alfie Ling hurried into the room.

"Now, calm down, sir!" he said to Mr Greengage who had jumped from his seat and was towering above Clara.

"You need to arrest him, Constable Ling," Clara said quietly, trying to keep her fear buttoned tightly inside. "He killed his wife."

Looking a little baffled, Alfie Ling came forward and took Mr. Greengage by the arm.

"She betrayed me!" Mr Greengage beat his chest with his hand. "She took my last strand of sanity, she killed herself, really, she did!"

Ling's look of bafflement had faded to one of calm professionalism.

"I think you best come with me sir." He drew Mr Greengage to the door.

"No!" The old man shouted. "No! Don't make me go outside! No! No! Not again, I can't, I can't."

Mr Greengage was writhing in Ling's hands.

"He was like this on the day we had to move him across the road to tend to Mrs Greengage." Ling scowled and, with a final shove, he had Mr. Greengage outside, where he stood in the snow and wept.

"Take his coat, you fool!" Clara snapped at Ling, running to Mr Greengage and draping a grey jacket over his shoulders. Then she whispered to him. "Don't be afraid."

"I wish I had died out there. I wish I never came home." Mr Greengage sobbed.

A few neighbours had opened their windows to ogle the scene with curiosity. Clara cast a scowl at them, but in truth she knew she would have done the same had the matter been occurring in her own street.

"It'll be all right now." She soothed the frail old man who looked a world away from being a killer once more, if she had not seen that shock of temper within him, she never would have believed her own theory. He was the farthest thing she could imagine from being the 'murdering-type'.

"Now, sir, it's a bit of a walk." Alfie Ling took Mr Greengage's arm and led him out of the garden.

The old man trembled and cowered at each sound – the click of the gate, the bark of a neighbour's dog, the dull thud of snow falling from tree branches – and looked more like a spooked rabbit than a human. Clara followed quietly. She wondered if policemen always felt so sick and hollow when they found their culprit, or whether it was just her. Perhaps she wasn't cut out for this business after all, not when the answers she sought so hard proved so painful. Justice seemed far away at that moment.

Chapter Twenty-Nine

"C heer up, old thing," Tommy squeezed her hand.

They were walking down North Street, heading through the town and out into the remains of the fields beyond. Tommy had finally figured out all the riddles, or at least he thought he had. There still seemed an awful lot of leeway and compromise in his decryptions for Clara's tastes, but they had kept him busy during the days when the snow was too thick to let him out the house, so she was at least grateful for that.

It was now a week since the arrest of Mr Greengage, and a warm spell of weather had reduced the snow to an icy layer of an inch or so. Tommy refused to be cooped up in the house any longer and, with the riddles solved, he was desperate to go off treasure hunting.

Annie had been characteristically appalled at her patient's determination and had made her usual protests and obtained the usual platitudes and brush-offs from Tommy, who more than ever was dying to get outside and enjoy the world at large. He threatened to push his own wheelchair if no one would help him, and after almost tipping himself over trying to get out the front door, it was agreed it was safer to give in to his request then to ignore it.

Now he was wrapped in a thick sweater and coat, gloves, scarf and hat – all appeasements to Annie, who had also insisted on preparing a stone hot water bottle that she had somehow balanced and strapped to the footrests of his chair.

Tommy had restrained his resistance to these measures for the greater good, a part of which was getting Clara out of the house. She had not gone to her office in the last week, claiming the weather too bad, which seemed feeble even to Annie. She was depressed in spirits, and Tommy understood the cause, having listened to the entire story of Mr Greengage's confession on the day of the arrest. What he didn't understand was how his sister could feel guilty. She had done her duty, she had not made Mr Greengage a murderer and clearly the man was unstable. How could she feel sorry for him? It would be like Tommy feeling guilty over the Germans he had shot in the war. He knew some men did, he knew it tore them apart, but for him it had all become crystal clear the moment he stepped out of a trench. You shot them or they shot you. There was no place for guilt.

He supposed it was being a woman that made Clara feel things so deeply. He was beginning to suspect she was on the verge of giving up being a private investigator entirely and he knew if she did it would be the biggest mistake she could make.

So his treasure hunt was partly fuelled by his own excitement and partly by his desire to get Clara out and about and thinking again. The only downside was that she had insisted on letting Mrs Wilton know about the plan and the woman had invited herself along.

"You do look rather dismal, dear," the woman now said as she heard Tommy's comment, "Anyone would think you hadn't solved this case at all, instead of bringing a murderer to justice."

"Is it justice though?" Clara was half-lost in her own thoughts. "He is a poor old man, it hardly seems justice to lock him away."

"He shot his wife," Mrs Wilton said steadily.

"I know, I just… oh, I don't know how I feel."

"It's the weather." Mrs Wilton said with the certainty of the ignorant, "Now when will you be back at work? I've told all my friends about you and they want to bring you their problems."

"I'm not sure…"

"She'll be back on Monday," Tommy interrupted his sister. She glared at him.

"Jolly good, I'll let them know. I must say this is quite exciting. A treasure hunt! I haven't down such a thing since I was a girl. I do hope we have the right spot. Is there any doubt?"

"None," Tommy said confidently.

"Oh, this is simply exhilarating."

Clara had other words for their adventure including cold and boring, but she was biting her tongue for everyone's sake. She knew she had been rather gloomy of late and didn't want to spoil the day for Tommy. He had been so proud to crack the riddles; she only hoped they found something and that Mrs Greengage wouldn't prove the old con-artist Clara suspected she was.

They passed out of the main town and into the quieter roads.

"Now if you will look at the map." Tommy wrenched off a glove using his teeth and unfolded a large sheet of paper. Annie tutted.

"I've marked the sites I believe the riddles refer to," Tommy said, spitting out the glove. "That is the ruined church, riddle no.6."

He pointed over the field.

"I shan't go over the earlier clues that led me to this stage, suffice it to say they referred to various spots within the town. I chose Mrs Wilton's house as a starting point, because it seemed logical that her husband would expect to lead her from there."

Clara felt like interjecting some comment on the nonsense of it all, but decided she would only sound catty and kept her mouth shut.

"Now, a little further on is Muggett's field." Tommy was indicating red crosses on his map. "After that we have to leave the road."

Annie let out an exasperated gasp.

"It isn't far," Tommy promised, trying to twist backwards and look up into Annie's face.

"At least all this pushing keeps me warm," Annie muttered.

"I'll help, Annie, I can take one handle." Clara offered.

"Oh no miss." Annie looked shocked. "That is not fit, not in front of a guest."

Clara blushed as though she had been scolded.

"That's Muggett's field!" Mrs Wilton yelled out in excitement, almost running up the road to reach it first. "I know this place, my dear husband and I used to come here when we were courting and look at the cows that used to be kept here. They were milkers, and were as friendly as a dog. We even named some."

Mrs Wilton stared across the icy field lost in her own memories.

"Even if we don't find treasure, we've made her day," Tommy winked at Clara.

She managed to smile. Watching Mrs Wilton's excitement was beginning to cheer her.

"You have to go back to work, old thing," Tommy added.

Clara looked at him sharply.

"I know a dark humour when I see it, old girl, I get it enough." Tommy grinned at her. "But you can't give in to it. You wouldn't let me mope, would you?"

She had no time to answer as they were at the gate and Mrs. Wilton was eager for the next clue.

"We head for that rotted barn," Tommy said, "until we see a large stone; at least I think that was what the riddle meant. It will be distinctive, and then we head left."

"That will be right through a field," grumbled Annie. Tommy pretended not to hear her.

They marched along a rutted, frozen track that was used as a local shortcut by everyone who came this way, their eyes peeled for a distinctive looking stone.

"I think I need to have words with this Mr Wilton," Annie muttered as she forced the wheelchair over the hard ground.

Clara felt herself smiling more. She was starting to enjoy herself.

"A big rock!" Mrs Wilton cried out excitedly. "This way!"

And now they were marching over pasture ground awaiting its springtime tenants and Mrs Wilton was so far ahead that when she came to the next marking point Tommy had worked out, she was beyond it before he could call to her.

"Towards the lightning struck tree!" Tommy yelled and pointed.

Mrs Wilton fluttered and skipped like a girl to a ruined tree set to one side of the pasture. She was so eager that she reached inside the hollow tree to see if anything obvious had been hidden there and drew out her arm and gloved hand filthy with dirt and green grime.

"I feel like a little girl!" Mrs Wilton laughed at them, self-consciously showing her stained clothes. "I really am being such a fool, aren't I?"

"Enjoy yourself," Clara said and she meant it, if only everyone could be made so carefree by a silly game of riddles.

"I think you'll find we have to dig," Tommy interrupted.

"Yes, I suspected that when I saw the shovels." Clara looked on forlornly as Annie unstrapped a bundle from the back of the wheelchair. She gave Clara a long-suffering look and deposited two shovels on the ground.

"Oh, let me, I used to be quite the gardener," Mrs Wilton grabbed a shovel and began ploughing her way enthusiastically into the soil.

Clara watched her for a moment and then sighed and picked up the remaining tool. The ground was frozen hard and difficult to dig, but Mrs Wilton's excitement spurred them on. She talked all the time about the savings her husband had and all his investments and how, now she was to have his money, she would do up the old house, fix the plumbing at long last and take to having a fire lit in more than one room at a time. She made no mention of dismissing Elaine, Clara noted, she wondered what the story was between those two.

But as the ground yielded inch by steady inch with no obvious signs of anything beneath it the talk subsided. Mrs. Wilton's smile began to fade to a determined frown and she dug like a fury, but it seemed her effort was in vain. As the hole widened and deepened, and Annie took a turn with the shovel it slowly dawned on everyone there might be nothing there.

Clara took a break, her arms burning and her palms blistered, to stand behind Tommy's wheelchair and observe the proceedings. Mrs Wilton could not be persuaded to stop despite it becoming more and more apparent she was not about to find a hidden treasure.

"I was so sure," Tommy said sadly.

"You really believed in it, didn't you?" Clara said kindly.

"I did, I... I liked the idea of there being a pattern to all of this business, that somehow goodness would shine through. I liked the idea that someone in Heaven was watching over us, even just our dead relatives."

Clara watched the heartbreak forming on Mrs Wilton's face as finally she too began to realise she was not about to strike gold. Suddenly this adventure seemed a very bad idea.

"I wish I had never allowed this expedition," Clara sighed.

A chill wind had started to blow over the pasture and it swept aside her scarf. She turned to gather it and glimpsed someone at the hedge. She stopped and looked longer. It could have been a passing walker, or a labourer curious at the mess they were making. It could have been anyone at that distance, but the long coat and the dark hair seemed all too much of a coincidence.

Clara took two paces across the field and then paused. Would he run now? Why had he followed them here when Mrs Greengage's killer was captured?

She shielded her eyes from the low sunlight of the afternoon with one hand and studied the young man at the edge of the pasture. He was not watching her, but staring at the digging party. She couldn't tell at this distance what the expression on his face was, but he seemed interested. Plucking up her courage she marched across the hard grass.

She was nearly upon him when he looked up.

"Don't run." She immediately stood still, as if she had just stumbled on a wild bird and didn't want it taking off in fright.

He was younger than she had realised when she saw him close to, but there was a haggardness about his mouth and eyes that aged him. She knew that look. Tommy had worn it often enough.

"You've been following me," she said carefully.

"I didn't mean any harm." He was politely spoken.

"I know, so why did you do it?"

His eyes wandered across the pasture again.

"You don't know what it is to feel a stranger in your own town. To hear people say you were dead and not recognise you. War does that to you. Sometimes you want to go back so bad, but your feet won't let you because you are scared of the look people will give you when you see them at last."

"Who are you?" Clara asked.

"Can I come in and join your party?" The young man had not taken his eyes off the diggers.

"I don't know. I'm not sure about you."

"I won't ever follow you again." He looked at her and promised solemnly. "I only did it because I was plucking up my courage. Can you understand? You were the closest I could get, you were like a link until I was ready."

Stiffly he held out his hand.

"I'm Edward Wilton."

Clara shook his hand, feeling stunned but also delighted.

"Mrs Wilton's son?"

"Yes."

"It was thought you were dead."

"I'm not." Edward sighed. "But I was in a German prison camp for two long years. Someone must have muddled my dog tags. I finally got back here and it seemed all so... so... so familiar, so the same. I felt like a trespasser stepping back into Brighton with all these dark memories I have stored up here."

He tapped the side of his head.

"I felt I was disturbing something, that I would ruin what little was left of the goodness of Britain. Do you see?"

"Yes." Clara understood well. "My brother was in the war also."

"The gentleman in the wheelchair?"

"Yes."

Edward Wilton abruptly looked at his feet and turned away slightly.

"I'm sorry if I scared you. I wasn't sure why mum had gone to you, I thought she might be looking for me and I had this idea I could come to you and you would make all the introductions that I couldn't. But it didn't work like that. I lost my nerve."

"Never mind that now, you must come and see your mother."

"Do... do you think she'll want to see me?" Edward glanced at his mother who was finally putting up her shovel in defeat. "It's been a long time and I've changed. Will she want me back like this?"

Edward was utterly terrified at the thought of being rejected and he was close to walking away and leaving Brighton for good rather than risk facing that possibility. Clara reached out and took his hand.

"She *will* want to see you." She pulled him through the gap in the hedge and, securely holding his hand, led him back to her small party.

Tommy glanced up first, looking baffled. But Clara winked at him, so he said nothing. Annie was grumbling about ruining her coat for nothing and trying to find where she had placed the packets of sandwiches she had made, while Mrs. Wilton had wedged her shovel in the ground and was standing staring at the hole. Tears were trickling down her cheeks.

Edward broke from Clara's grasp.

"Mother?"

Mrs Wilton jerked from her thoughts. For a moment she looked over blankly and then her expression softened and her body sagged.

"Edward? But it can't be?" She stepped forward but she was afraid he would fade away if she touched him.

"There was a mistake, mother, I never died." Edward reached out his hand.

Mrs Wilton was trembling. Very daintily she took it, then with a great sob she threw herself into her son's arms and clutched him tight.

"You came back! You came back!"

Edward wrapped his arms around her and felt his own burdens lifted. He had been accepted.

"No wonder Mrs Greengage couldn't contact him, he wasn't dead!" Tommy said jovially, biting into a very cold egg sandwich Annie had handed out.

"Mrs Greengage was nothing but a charlatan, as those riddles surely prove," Clara replied firmly.

"Really?" Tommy grinned. "Seems to me Mrs Wilton found a greater treasure in this field today than she ever could have imagined."

"Tommy!" Clara snorted in exasperation. "That is pure coincidence!"

Tommy gave her one of his most infuriating smiles, the one that made her feel as though he knew a big secret and wasn't telling. She wanted to thump him.

"Coincidence is just a word cynics use when they don't want to believe in fate, or miracles."

Clara rolled her eyes.

"Fine, don't believe me." Tommy smirked. "But here we are, at this very moment, having followed a series of random riddles, to this very spot, I might add, just at the same moment as master Wilton chose to appear."

"He's been following me, that's all."

"Not recently he hasn't, so why did he start again today? Why not yesterday, or tomorrow?"

"Eat your egg sandwich." Clara groaned. "You spend too much time with your head in books."

Tommy let the matter rest, but she saw him looking at her out of the corner of his eye the entire time they were heading home with the Wiltons trailing behind them. She concluded that having a brother could be exceedingly infuriating.

Chapter Thirty

"**M**r Greengage will get his first hearing next week, but I am not sure it will ever get to trial. I've got doctors everywhere telling me his sanity is questionable and that he wouldn't be able to stand up in court. Even if he does it looks like it will be a lunatic asylum for him rather than prison." Inspector Park-Coombs scratched at his chin as he chatted to Clara. "Biscuit?"

He offered her a plate and Clara took one reluctantly. She had not been eating properly since the arrest of Mr Greengage and Annie had been nagging her about her loss of weight. She nibbled the edge of the biscuit.

"I still feel so guilty," she said.

"Why? He was a killer? All right, his mind isn't all there and someone should have been called in to see him sooner, but that was private business not ours. We are just here to mop up the messes, not try to prevent them."

Clara looked at him mournfully.

"Do you really think like that?"

The inspector sighed and munched into a piece of shortbread.

"You feel sorry for the fellow, he looks meek and vulnerable, but something went snap inside him and he crossed a line. Over a parrot

I might add." He brushed crumbs from his waistcoat. "My men have heard him talking to it sometimes, you know? When no one is around."

Clara shook her head.

"Have you never felt bitter inside for finding out the truth?" she asked. "Have you never wondered if you had done the right thing?"

"A lot of policemen will tell you that ain't your business, you just do your duty." The inspector frowned. "But you have to be a pretty cold bugger for that, excuse my French."

"What is the alternative?"

"You always remember that as much as you feel sorry for a killer, as much as you sympathise, there is one other person who deserves your sympathy far more – the victim. Because they are dead and gone, we tend to forget them after a while, we keep on dealing with the living and they slip away. But their life was cut short, stolen from them. They had no choice. The killer always has a choice."

Clara let that sink in. Had she forgotten about Mrs Greengage in all the confusion of the case?

"Maybe this will help." Park-Coombs pushed a brown cardboard folder towards her. "It's all the background information we dug up on her. You look it over while I make a fresh pot of tea."

Reluctantly Clara opened the file, she felt she already had a fair grasp of the domineering Mrs Greengage, she had after all spoken with the Bundles, her neighbours and, of course, her husband. What more could she know?

She read the first entry.

Born 1872, daughter of a lace-maker. Only child of ten to survive to adulthood. Mother died of alcoholism, father ran off with another woman when she was fourteen. Unknown how she spent her years before meeting Frederick Greengage, mill worker. Married within six months.

Clara stared at it with astonishment, could someone's life have been so dramatic in such a short space of time? She read on carefully.

Pregnant 1889, lost the child. Frederick made unemployed, former colleagues suggest he was stealing to supplement his income and to try and provide enough for Martha. She takes on piece work for a milliner's shop and is said to have persuaded Frederick to try performing on the stage.

Between 1890 and 1892 Frederick and Martha live in poverty, frequently without a roof over their heads. Frederick is heavily in debt.

1893 Frederick appears on stage as 'Gassy Greengage' a comedian and magician. Shortly after he is briefly arrested under suspicion the suit he was wearing was stolen, case cannot be proved. Martha has a daughter, Josephine. Frederick continues performing and the family fortunes improve.

1894 – 1897 Frederick's stage career takes off. Martha, however, is taken ill with suspected phosphorous poisoning from producing homemade matches to supplement their income. Josephine dies in the winter.

Frederick and Martha move around the country from theatre to theatre. Frederick now has a larger performance, but Martha is said to have been deeply miserable (NB. Gossip from other stage performers) and still frail from her illness. In 1900 she has a son, George, but six months later is found in a daze having apparently tried to kill herself with laudanum.

In 1905 they are still travelling when George dies as a result of a carriage accident. Frederick is widely said to have blamed Martha and from then on they rarely spent time in each other's company. Between 1906 – 1912 Frederick is rumoured to have had numerous romances with fellow stage performers, one lady is said to have become pregnant, but no proof. In 1913 Frederick develops a long-term romance with a

*female performer (NB. Referred to as 'Olive' but could be stage-name)
who becomes pregnant but doesn't want the child. Frederick tries to
persuade Martha to claim the child as their own, apparently this tips
her over the edge again and another suicide attempt is made, this time
by drowning. Distraught Frederick breaks off the affair with 'Olive' and
friends heard him to declare he would do anything to win back Martha.*

*The marriage remains miserable, on the outbreak of war Frederick
states to friends that Martha cannot stand him any longer and he will
join up to prove himself. Frederick leaves for war in 1914 and does not
return until 1917 when invalided out. From then on he is a recluse and
Martha has to find work, this time as a clairvoyant.*

After that the story played out as Clara knew. She settled back the
file on the desk and let her mind wander over the details. So Frederick
Greengage was not quite the saintly, under-the-thumb husband she
had imagined. Martha, whose life had been constantly tarnished with
poverty and desperation, must have been deeply aggrieved when the
man she couldn't stand, who had disgraced her, came back a nervous
wreck who she then had to nurse. More than that, she supported him.
She could have walked out and left him, no one would have blamed
her after all his philandering, but instead she took care of him.

Clara sat back in her chair. This was a very different Mrs Greengage
to the one she had thought she knew. It explained her seeming
hardness, her cut-throat nature. She had learned to survive however
she could.

Inspector Park-Coombs returned with the teapot, he was warming
his hands on the sides, the room was chilly.

"Did it answer a few things?"

"Certainly," Clara said. "As much as I dislike some of her actions
I can see why Martha Greengage was who she was. Frederick was a
difficult husband."

"It might also interest you to know that since we typed up that report we learned that 'Olive' was probably the same lady as Mrs. Bundle. It seems she had dabbled on the stage before meeting her husband."

"But the dates?"

"Yes, it seems she was having an extra-marital affair too and one of her children is probably the child Frederick told his wife about."

Clara shook her head.

"Then her accusations were all part of a terrible revenge, but against the wrong people."

"The real culprit was dead." The inspector shrugged. "I doubt Mrs Greengage was thinking straight. Her husband had returned a shattered soul, she was struggling to keep the house together and there was the woman he had run off with apparently with everything. It was a mean-spirited act, for sure, but she needed to lash out at someone."

The inspector poured out fresh, hot cups of tea.

"Do you understand now what I mean about remembering the victim when you feel sorry for the murderer?"

"I think I do. I still feel Mrs Greengage was a wicked woman for the games she played with people, but she didn't deserve to be shot. Perhaps the parrot really was sick and she was trying to be kind."

"We'll never know." The inspector sighed. "Now, while I am on the matter I want to discuss our, shall we say, working relationship."

Clara raised an eyebrow.

"I beg your pardon?"

"This case has raised your profile and I expect you will find yourself handling more of these sorts of crimes soon."

"I have no intention of taking on a murder case again!"

The inspector grinned.

"Well, let's just say, if you do, I would like to think you would liaise with the police so we could share resources. On occasion a private individual can winkle out details the police cannot. We are rather official looking and people do not talk freely to us."

"From now on I am sticking to mundane cases," Clara said determinedly.

"Be that as it may," smiled the inspector, "I had this prepared in case you changed your mind."

He pushed a card towards her, it read;

"Miss C. Fitzgerald. Private advisor to the police. Authorised Access, confirmed by Inps. W. Park-Coombs."

"It means you can stick your nose in anywhere around here once I have given permission."

Clara handled the card suspiciously.

"You really do think I will be handling more murder cases, don't you?"

"Not just that. Robberies, frauds, you name it."

Clara shook her head.

"You really are mistaken Inspector. I will turn away anyone who asks me to investigate criminal cases from now on," she said firmly.

Yet, as she was leaving, the inspector couldn't help noticing she put the card carefully in her bag.

Enjoyed this Book?

You can make a difference

As an independent writer reviews of my books are hugely important to help my work reach a wider audience. If you haven't already, I would love it if you could take five minutes to review this book on Amazon.

Thank you very much!

The Clara Fitzgerald Series

Have you read them all?

Murder and Mascara

The ninth mystery

The Green Jade Dragon

The tenth mystery

The Monster at the Window

The eleventh mystery

Murder on the Mary Jane

The twelfth mystery

The Missing Wife

The thirteenth mystery

The Traitor's Bones

The fourteenth mystery

The Fossil Murder

The fifteenth mystery

Mr Lynch's Prophecy

The sixteenth mystery

Death at the Pantomime

The seventeenth mystery

The Cowboy's Crime

The eighteenth mystery

The Trouble with Tortoises

The nineteenth mystery

The Valentine Murder

The twentieth mystery

A Body Out of Time

The twenty-first mystery

The Dog Show Affair

The twenty-second mystery

The Unlucky Wedding Guest

The twenty-third mystery

Also by Evelyn James

The Gentleman Detective Series

The Gentleman Detective

Norwich 1898.

Colonel Bainbridge, private detective, is wondering if it is time to hang up his magnifying glass when the arrival of his niece and the unexpected death of a pugilist has him trying to prove a man innocent of murder.

Delving into the murky world of street fighting and match fixing, can they determined who really killed the boxer Simon One-Foot or will a man who has done no wrong end up swinging for a crime he could not have committed?

Available on Amazon

About the Author

Evelyn James (aka Sophie Jackson) began her writing career in 2003 working in traditional publishing before embracing the world of ebooks and self-publishing. She has written over 80 books, available on a variety of platforms, both fiction and non-fiction.

You can find out more about Sophie's various titles at her website **www.sophie-jackson.com** or connect through social media on Facebook **www.facebook.com/SophieJacksonAuthor** and if you fancy sending an email do so at **sophiejackson.author@gmail.com**

Printed in Great Britain
by Amazon

47660408R00138